Fall Me Maybe

LANEY HATCHER

Print Edition
ISBN: 979-8-9910786-0-3

Fall Me Maybe

CHAPTER 1

Noah

The life of a Huber driver. That's *Huber*, with an "H."

I'd only been doing this gig for two weeks, but I already had a routine. I vacuumed the back seat and the floorboards daily. In case any of my fares got thirsty, I kept tiny bottles of water in the front seat in an old Igloo cooler I'd found at a thrift store. Jimmy Huber—my new boss—told me it was a waste of time to make customers comfortable, but I thought people liked it. Sometimes just the offer made someone smile.

I worked the evening and night shifts for Jimmy six days a week in Cozy Creek, Colorado. I was one of only two drivers. Henry preferred the morning and daytime shifts, and I didn't have the motivation or the seniority to fight him on them. Jimmy pulled an occasional shift as needed, and for the most part, the three of us had this tiny tourist town handled as far as ride-shares went.

See, we only drove for the locals. It was a Jimmy rule. And with the way his operation worked, there wasn't really a way for outsiders to contact us unless they knew someone in town. And even then, Jimmy was very picky about who we picked up. All ride-share requests went through him—in the most technologically offensive way possible, but whatever. I wasn't in charge here. I just drove my Bronco and picked up locals as instructed. I needed this job if I was going to save up enough money to uproot again.

Cozy Creek was inundated with tourists several months out of the year, or so I'd been told. It was an idyllic little town that drew skiers and snowboarders in the winter—people with money to burn on the nearby slopes. Out-of-towners also flocked to my brand-new town during autumn to check out the fall foliage and small-town entertainment. Cozy Creek was the best, worst-kept secret in Colorado. Or at least that was what this famous social media influencer once said, and now the town had it plastered on all their marketing materials.

It seemed nice, so far. I was used to the whole small-town thing. I was from a rural speed bump over in eastern South Carolina. But the difference was, my hometown was dead and dying. There was no tourism to revive it. Factories closing and little commerce to speak of, the streets and neighborhoods of Baxter, South Carolina, looked bleak when compared to the bright, shiny Main Street I was currently driving down.

Two weeks wasn't really enough time to get settled. But I

hadn't brought much with me to Cozy Creek. I'd sold off most of my things and made the twenty-nine-hour drive across the middle of the country to start a new life. Expectation hadn't really meshed with reality, but that wasn't the town's fault. So, here I was, making the best out of a twisted situation while I saved money and collected my shredded pride. Driving a *Huber*.

My upcoming rider was one point two miles away at the Shady Peaks apartment complex, just outside of downtown. Following my vehicle's navigation, I made it through a traffic light and turned into the parking lot where a collection of buildings sat, each rising four stories into the deep blue sky. It looked nice and well-tended, and most of the cars in the lot were firmly middle class.

A woman stood on the sidewalk in a pale orange dress. She ignored the bench behind her and, instead, stood staring down at her phone, with what appeared to be an iced coffee in hand.

Quickly glancing at my own phone mounted on the dashboard, I checked the name of my rider and then slowed my approach as I regarded the pint-sized woman tapping the toe of her leopard-print ballet flat on the concrete. No one else was around, so this had to be my next ride.

My eyes narrowed as I took in the riot of long wavy blond hair around her face—a face that appeared youthful and at odds with my current expectations. She looked to be around my age. Maybe slightly younger than my own twenty-seven years.

My approach didn't divert her attention from the screen of her phone, however. Her fingers clutched the rainbow case in a death grip.

It was early September and a gorgeous seventy-one degrees Fahrenheit, so my windows were already down. I cleared my throat, not wanting to startle the girl. "Um, hi. I think I'm here to pick you up. Are you Luanne Billings?"

The woman's head jerked up at my announcement, and wide gray eyes met mine before she winced. "Please call me Lu. Lu-anne is a sixty-five-year-old woman with a beehive who chain-smokes Virginia Slims. I'm twenty-five and, well . . . none of those things."

She slid her phone inside her giant purse and hoisted it onto her shoulder.

"So you prefer Marlboro, then?" I teased.

She laughed and produced some sunglasses from some-where—probably the bodybag slung over her arm. "No, I don't smoke." Her gray eyes were still smiling, right along with the rest of her as she walked around to the rear passenger-side door and climbed in, sliding the shades on her face. "And my beehive is in the shop."

I bit down on my grin as I waited for the sound of her seat belt to click into place. Pulling up my navigation, I input her destina-tion. It was a restaurant on the outskirts of town. I hadn't been there yet, and from all the little dollar signs below the search results, I couldn't afford it even if I wanted to.

"So you're new," my passenger stated from the back seat as I checked my mirrors and eased away from the curb. It wasn't phrased as a question, but I'd been getting the same version of it from curious residents since I started working for Jimmy.

"Yeah, I took over for Zoe." It was the answer I'd been handing out to everyone, a shiny offering to distract and keep them at a distance.

Shortly after my disastrous arrival, I'd seen the job posting on a corkboard in the coffee shop downtown for a local car service. I'd called the number on the flyer and interviewed with Jimmy the same day.

Jimmy Huber was a no-nonsense ex-cabby from Manhattan. He'd driven for over forty years before retiring to Colorado where he had family—a sister and two nieces. Cozy Creek was too small to support Uber or Lyft employees the way a bigger town might, and the locals occasionally needed rides in, out, and around town. He'd seen a need and used his experience to create something completely unhinged and ridiculous but profitable.

Riders called Jimmy with requests, and he texted his drivers their pickup and drop-off details. If something came up and we couldn't make it, Jimmy took the fare himself. But that was pretty rare. Henry—the dayshift Huber driver—loved driving and listening to audiobooks in his car. And I was too poor to turn down any income thrown my way. Riders paid in cash at the end of their ride. Even after hearing that Huber had been up and running for over eight years, I honestly couldn't believe the whole thing worked as smoothly as it did, but I was two weeks in, and nothing strange had come up yet. And I was making enough at an hourly rate from Jimmy and my tips from riders to get me back on my feet and hopefully on my way.

"Oh, she had the baby already?" Lu asked as she put some lipstick on using my mirror to check her reflection.

I focused on her question and tried not to be distracted by the shape of her lips or the bright red she deftly streaked across them. "Not yet, but soon, I think."

I still felt a little weird about replacing Zoe. Jimmy's gruff voice and Brooklyn accent informed me at my interview that he needed to find someone to take over the young woman's shifts. "She's pregnant with her second kid, and the first car seat was already taking up too much room in the back seat," he'd said. I'd tried really hard not to make a face at that and figured I'd mostly succeeded because I got the job and started picking people up the following day. He'd explained that the service was for locals only but occasionally residents would tell a friend or family member visiting from out of town about us. And apparently, that was okay as long as Jimmy liked them.

I was pretty much trying to stay on Jimmy's good side, what with the aforementioned poverty.

"So what's your name, New Zoe?" Lu's voice rose over the rush of fresh air blowing in through the windows.

I peeked in the rearview mirror to find her smiling with those red lips and blond hair blowing all around. "I'm Noah," I replied, quickly looking away. The restaurant was up ahead on the right.

"Are you new to town? Or just passing through?"

I cleared my throat, focusing on driving and answering with the same response I'd given to everyone else who'd asked. "I'm new. Only been here a couple of weeks so far." It was really hard to get a job when people thought you were temporary. So I hadn't advertised my plans to be on my way to anyone. Maybe that was dishonest. But, again, see above: poverty.

Lu made a soft hum I almost missed with the breeze, but then she asked, "So what made you move here? Cozy Creek is pretty small and out of the way."

I hesitated and found her scrutinizing me in the rearview mirror. She wore sunglasses, and I couldn't see her eyes, but I could feel her attention like a sunlamp warming my skin.

Huffing out a little laugh, I admitted, "It's kind of embarrassing."

I didn't know why I'd told her that. I hadn't confessed as much to the other nosy Cozy Creek residents who'd asked.

"Oh, reallllly?" Now, I had her full attention. The prospect was both distressing and electrifying. She had a cool-girl vibe, like the pretty, popular head cheerleader from high school. Being the center of her focus now made me feel like a bumbling loser by comparison.

"Let me guess." She tapped her chin thoughtfully. "You're a beekeeper—"

"An apiarist," I interrupted.

"Really?"

I chuckled. "Yes, that's what they're called."

"Why do you know that?"

"I don't know. I just remembered it from something I read."

"Okay, nerd," she said, causing me to burst out laughing in surprise. When was the last time someone had teased me? It had been a while.

"You're a beekeeper," she repeated. "And moved here to work out at Sutton Farms, but you realized too late that you are deathly allergic to bees."

"But not *too,* too late," I countered.

She nodded. "Clearly. You're still breathing."

Her ridiculous statement drew another laugh out of me and she preened in the back seat as a result, those red lips framing even, white teeth. "No, that's not it. But close."

Lu's grin went supernova. "I'll just keep guessing."

That sobered me a little, and I returned my focus to the road. I doubted she'd be able to guess how I ended up in Cozy Creek. I sure as shit hadn't seen it coming myself.

"Well, it's nice to meet you, Noah," she called into the quiet between us before my sudden silence could make it too awkward. "I'm sure we'll be seeing more of each other."

"Oh, yeah?" I wondered, somewhat disquieted by the prospect.

"My car is in the shop," she explained.

"I thought it was your beehive."

Another laugh. This girl was friendly. She sounded like she laughed a lot, the sound easy and free, her lips shaping her grin effortlessly. But I still got a warm feeling in my chest that I'd amused her and drawn that bright, happy sound out. The sunlamp sensation spread at a distressing rate.

"My beehive and my SUV both," she confirmed, still smiling.

Slowing, I turned on my signal and pulled close to the restaurant door. The parking lot was full, and a few well-dressed people crossed in front of me to enter.

"Why Lu?" I asked suddenly before I could stop myself. There was no real reason to ask beyond curiosity. I nearly cursed myself out loud. It was dangerous to be curious about anyone here. "Why not Anne or Annie or a middle name since the beehive doesn't fit?"

She stayed quiet for a moment, still buckled up in the back seat despite being parked at the entrance. "I don't know. I've always just been Lu. My mom called me that since I was a baby."

Not moving, Lu still stared out the window, so I prompted, "Is there anything else I can help you with?"

She finally turned to meet my gaze in the mirror. "I just need a minute. First-date jitters."

So she was going on a date at this fancy restaurant. "Oh, yeah. Sure." I rubbed my palms down the legs of my jeans, ignoring disappointment I didn't have any business feeling—for a variety of complicated reasons.

Lu eventually pulled off her sunglasses and tucked them back into the cavern of her big leather purse. She let loose a long breath before passing me the cash for her fare. After thanking me, she climbed out of the car to stand next to my window on the sidewalk. After a sip of her nearly empty iced coffee, she said with a grin, "I'll see you around, Noah."

My grip tightened on my steering wheel as I forced myself to look at her. She was pretty, I realized. Objectively so. All ready for her date in her pretty fall sweater dress. Seeing her and that bright smile and killer red lipstick, it was hard to ignore how beautiful she was. But there was something else—something approachable and friendly in her loose hair and those laugh lines that hinted at how often she found a smile.

Clearing my throat, I said quickly, "Yeah, see you around, Luanne."

A perfectly arched dark-blond eyebrow rose. "None of that, beekeeper."

I allowed the small smile I'd been fighting, reluctant to admit that she was pretty and funny and apparently a single person who dated. "Sorry. Sorry. Good night, Lu."

I was done being charmed by women. If I needed a reminder about why, I only needed to take a helpful gander at my new surroundings.

I refused to let myself think about red lips or wild blond hair or quick-witted Lu. She was a stranger. I didn't know her. And sometimes even when you *thought* you knew someone, you didn't. Not enough to trust them, anyway.

Maybe I'd see her again. If, like she'd said, her car was in for repairs. She'd be just another local calling for a Huber.

I didn't allow myself to wonder if she'd be okay in there. Or to question how she'd get home without her car. And it definitely wasn't my place to wonder if she'd go home with whomever awaited her inside. It wasn't my place to wonder about her at all.

Making my way back toward Main Street, I decided I'd stay central to town in case another ride request came in from Jimmy. I took in the shiny shop windows and the people walking the brick sidewalks in their flannel and puffy vests. They looked happy and eager to soak in the magic of autumn. Gourds and sunflowers decorated many of the entryways while bright yellow, red, and purple mums swung from hanging baskets on every lamppost. The Rockies loomed in the background as the tourists stopped to take selfies and point at the architecture of the old buildings downtown.

A marquee in front of the visitor center advertised the upcoming pumpkin-judging contest next month, telling people to "Go Big or Gourd Home." I wondered if I'd still be driving people around town by then, tense as I scanned faces in the crowd. Would my one-bedroom apartment above the Cozy Creek Confectionery feel like home, or would I be packing up my meager possessions to start over again?

Twenty minutes later, at 7:14 p.m., a text came through from Jimmy. I blinked at the name on the request before cursing and making two left turns to head back the way I'd come.

Curiosity I had no business feeling worked its way under my skin as I drove.

The restaurant was in shadow as the sun had fallen behind the snowcapped mountains in the distance. Lu stood out front with her comically large purse dangling off her shoulder. She grinned as she watched me bring the Bronco to stop beside her.

"Fancy meeting you here, Louis Armstrong. Date over so soon?"

Somehow, her smile grew wider, and I had to wonder what had happened. Did the douchebag stand her up? She didn't seem too upset about it, regardless.

"Yeah, it didn't work out," was all she said as she hopped down onto the parking lot asphalt and went around to climb, once again, into the back seat. "But if you're hungry, I know a great place for burgers. My treat since I made you come right back and pick me up."

My brow furrowed in confusion along with an instinctual dose of suspicion. "You requested a ride. You're paying me. You don't have to thank me with food."

"Fine," she replied, unbothered. "Then I'll buy your silence about my dating fail tonight."

I took in her cheerful expression with reservation and, again, wondered what had gone on inside that restaurant.

"Burgers and bribes, Noah," she singsonged. "Come on."

She was so . . . ridiculous. But charming. And fascinating. I could feel myself being taken in by her. That sunlamp warmth lighting up my skin despite the growing darkness.

"Fine," I said, releasing a put-upon sigh. "But there better be tater tots."

I detected a sage nod from my rearview mirror. "Of course. Can't have a decent burger without tots." And then she smiled, full and flattering, like she knew she'd won and was used to things going her way.

Then I didn't care anymore about the loser who'd missed out tonight.

I could have a burger with a pretty stranger in this temporary layover of my current life. It didn't have to mean anything. And it definitely didn't indicate I was letting my guard down.

I had no plans to do that anytime soon.

CHAPTER 2

Lu

"Where to today, Lucy Liu?"

Six fifteen p.m. Right on time. My hero.

I grinned in response to Noah's Lu nickname. Apparently, this was our thing now. And I didn't see any reason to fight my amusement—not the way Noah did. I could feel his reluctance like a tangible thing.

Last night, when we'd gone for burgers at Skytop Diner after I'd gotten stood up by my asshole blind date, Noah had been very cautious with me. And maybe that was just part of meeting someone new and trying to gauge how crazy they were. Could be that was just Noah—reserved and guarded—but I didn't think so. His amazing hazel eyes would brighten at something I'd said before quickly looking away. His lips would twitch with the beginnings of a smile but then flatten back out as if he'd made a conscious decision to withhold his amusement, to appear unaffected.

Something told me that I'd have to earn it with this guy. He didn't trust easily or he'd been hurt somewhere along the way. Either way, I was a persistent little gremlin—he just didn't know it yet. And my instincts flared bright and loud, telling me that Noah needed a friend. He was new to town, after all. But more than that, I could see the sadness lingering over him like a storm cloud, and I wanted to help.

We'd had fun together. He was sharp and funny, and I'd liked him right away. I'd certainly had more fun on the short drive to the restaurant than waiting for some online match who had no respect for my time and had failed to show.

"Today," I said, finally responding to his question, "I'm going to a family dinner."

Tossing my purse in the back seat, I climbed into Noah's baby-blue Bronco and got situated.

Eyes flicking to mine in the rearview mirror, he said, "Why the face?"

Had I made a face? Probably. It was hard for me to keep my emotions to myself. And it was even more difficult to mask my feelings. Especially when they were complicated.

"Family dinners are complicated," I admitted. "My dad remarried when I was in high school, and my stepfamily . . . isn't my biggest fan. Today we are gathering to meet my stepsister's newest boyfriend."

I honestly didn't know what to expect. My stepsister, Ginny, was difficult to get close to. We were the same age and had been classmates since preschool. But we'd never been friends. It didn't stop me from trying, though. Besides, any opportunity to see my dad was never a wasted effort.

"Sorry," he mumbled awkwardly, hazel eyes back on the road as he left my apartment complex. "Families are tough. Just because the proximity is there doesn't mean the connection is."

"Yes. Exactly. Sometimes you have to really work to make those relationships stronger."

Noah's dark brows furrowed in the rearview mirror, but he didn't say anything.

"What?" I prompted, curious why he'd made that face. "You don't agree?"

His eyes touched mine briefly before flitting back to the road.

"You can tell me," I urged. "We're friends now. I introduced you to the best burger of your life. Our friendship is solidified in the annals for Cozy Creek fine dining."

"I wouldn't say the best burger of my life."

I made an affronted squawk that had him smiling, faint lines fanning out near his temples.

"Fine. It was the best burger I've ever had."

"Thank. You," I replied with an obnoxious amount of haughtiness, but his grin just widened. "Tell me what you're holding back. You disagree with what I said about families."

Noah sighed and flipped his blinker as we approached an intersection for the road my father lived on. "I just think that you shouldn't have to force it. Just because someone is related to you doesn't make you obligated to them." I opened my mouth to argue, but he continued as he drove slowly through the upper-middle-class neighborhood. "I'm not close with my parents. I visit on holidays and call every couple of months. And that was when we lived in the same town. They never made the effort to stay in my life as an adult, and that's fine, you know? They raised me. I was safe and warm and fed. But I get the sense that they saw me to my eighteenth birthday and then considered themselves done. Job finished. They have their own interests and lives and no desire to really know me as this adult version of the boy they raised."

I'd been watching him in the mirror the whole time he spoke, noting his frank honesty and unbothered expression, but he hadn't glanced up until now. "Hey, don't be sad. It's okay," he said in alarm.

That was so . . . so . . . awful. Why didn't Noah's parents try harder? Why didn't Noah? "Maybe you just need to work to let them know you as you are now. Then they'll see what an awesome person you are and want to be in your life for more than holidays and occasional phone calls."

"First of all, we just met. You don't know that I'm an awesome person. I could listen to Nickelback or use my speakerphone in public. And second of all, why should I have to work for it? Just because we share DNA? I wouldn't keep putting in the one-sided effort with, let's say, a friend from high school I'd grown apart from. I would probably let that relationship run its course."

I had no idea what to say. That was so counter to my entire life.

I'd been working hard to keep my family together for years—even with my aloof but well-meaning father and reluctant stepfamily.

"Lu, don't look so distraught." Noah laughed a little. "I feel like I broke you."

I cleared my throat, hoping to push away the uncomfortable emotion I felt. "No. I'm fine. You didn't."

"I just think that sometimes people don't deserve blind faith and dedication just because of blood. Holding on to the past like a lifeline only drags you backward. The effort of maintaining a relationship should go both ways and be equal. Not one person killing themselves to keep it all together."

Part of me could understand where he was coming from. But when you only had so much family left, it was important to protect it and maintain it. Otherwise, you'd just be . . . alone. A relationship with my family had been my goal for so long. I couldn't imagine giving up on it.

Hell, I'd been subjecting myself to online dating for the better part of a year to try to find a partner—a connection. I loved my hometown and my friends and my job. I just wanted *more*.

"That got surprisingly deep. I'm sorry. I didn't mean to overstep." Noah's low voice drew me out of the thoughts twisting me up unexpectedly on a Saturday evening.

"You didn't," I rushed to say. "I practically forced it out of you."

Noah slowed and pulled the Bronco into my father's driveway. Ginny's black BMW was parked in the middle and both my dad's and stepmom's vehicles were visible through the open garage door.

"Well, I hope your family dinner goes well. Hopefully, the new boyfriend is a decent guy."

"Thanks!" I replied brightly to make up for my strange and sour mood for the latter part of the drive. "I hope you have a good night, too. I'm sure you have to go and take care of the reason you moved here."

With his light brown hair a little disheveled from the wind, Noah spun in his seat to look at me. A teasing light shone in his expectant gaze. "And what reason is that?"

Deadpan, I replied, "Because you inherited that haunted mansion and have to stay there overnight in order to claim it."

"Yes, Scooby Doo. That is totally the reason I moved to Cozy Creek. You nailed it."

My grin claimed my features, stealing away the disquiet of our previous conversation. Noah's brilliant eyes tracked my amusement, and his own smile bloomed as well. And it felt all the more special because those grins were grudgingly given and few and far between. But my new goal, however futile, was drawing them out.

I liked his attention on me, so close in this confined space. Stealing fleeting glances in his rearview mirror made keeping a distance between us easy. But as he faced me, handsome features fully visible, that layer of protection suddenly stripped away, I felt the punch of attraction knock the breath out of me.

Gathering my things and my composure, I said, "I'll see you in a little while. Is nine okay? I already texted Jimmy."

"I'll be here, Lucifer."

I laughed delightedly and made my way inside my father's house, determined to hold on to the fizzy, happy feeling of Noah's teasing and his reluctant grin, even as I knew it couldn't get me through the next two hours.

The house was loud when I entered through the garage and into the mudroom off the kitchen. My stepmother's and stepsister's voices rose above the instrumental music my father played in the family room nearby.

I hadn't grown up in this house. Dad and Kimberly had moved here after they'd married the summer after my junior year of high school.

The home I'd shared with my mother and father was on the other side of Cozy Creek. A modest two-bedroom ranch with green shutters and a kitchen the size of a postage stamp. But I'd had fifteen years of love in that house. I'd learned how to ride a bike and then drive a car at the end of our cul-de-sac. There had been countless hours playing in the backyard—a lifetime ago. Cookie-making in our tiny kitchen. And learning how to paint with Mom at the dining table. Listening to records with Dad in his study. That life felt so distant now.

My mother died when I was fifteen. An aggressive cancer diagnosis hadn't given us long to prepare or say goodbye. I'd already been lost and adrift when my father had surprised me by dating and marrying Kimberly soon thereafter. He'd said he didn't like being alone—that he missed my mother too much. I figured that we must process grief differently because I wasn't looking for a replacement mother.

They'd married eight months after my mom died. My dad sold our family home, and we'd moved into Kimberly's mini mansion across town. She was a divorcée who volunteered at my high school and chaired the parent-teacher organization. I'd known her as Ginny Walker's well-dressed helicopter mom for as long as I could remember. But suddenly, she was my stepmother, and Ginny was supposed to be my stepsister instead of the most popular girl at school. Except she seemed to resent me for moving into her house and sharing her bathroom. Ginny didn't have a lot of sympathy as we were both forced to navigate this strange new situation. Her teasing and bullying escalated, and while she mostly ignored me at home, she and her cheerleader friends made my final year at Cozy Creek High School a living hell. She was always careful around my dad, so he never saw that side of her. And I'd been too afraid to rock the boat on my father's new-found happiness. So I'd kept my mouth shut. When graduation rolled around, I had been more than ready to pack up and attend Western Colorado University—several hours away—and live in the dorms.

But in escaping my stepsister, I'd missed out on time with my dad—my only remaining family member. If I didn't make an effort with Kimberly and Ginny, then I'd be all alone. Kimberly and I got along well enough. She wasn't antagonistic or anything. She just didn't really care about me.

I kept waiting for Ginny to grow up. To stop judging me and my clothes and my hair like we were still in high school. But here we were, both twenty-five years old, and still not any closer to being the blended family I was so desperate to make work. The jabs were subtler now and easier to withstand. It was important to me to have my dad in my life, so I kept the peace, made the effort, and hoped for the day it all paid off.

"Hi!" I said cheerfully to the room. Fake it till you make it, right?

My dad glanced up from the glass of wine he was pouring. "Hi, honey."

Kimberly and Ginny paused in their conversation so that my stepmother could murmur a polite hello.

Ginny turned her back and ignored me, picking up whatever thread they'd been discussing before I'd invaded their home. Something about a new car.

I pulled a bottle of wine out of my purse and deposited it on the counter before kissing my dad on the cheek.

Dad eyed the label and winced. "Would you like me to pour you a glass?"

"No, I brought it for Kimberly. It's from that vineyard in Aspen that she likes. I'll have a glass of whatever red you just poured."

Conversation once again paused before Ginny announced, "Mom isn't drinking right now. Bringing that in the house just tempts her, Lu. Great job."

My gaze shot to my stepmother, who looked pained, lines tight around her lips.

"Kimberly had some weird results come back in her blood work at her yearly checkup. Her doctor advised cutting back. She decided to give up wine before they test her again next month."

"Oh! I'm so sorry, Kimberly. I didn't realize. I'll just get rid of this," I offered, face flushing before I put the bottle back in my bag and hoisted it up on my shoulder.

As my stepmother remained quiet and tense, my dad shot me a sympathetic glance and passed me a glass of red wine—a grocery store brand and variety that Kimberly wouldn't touch with a ten-foot pole.

"Should we abstain with her, Dad? Isn't that insensitive?"

He shook his head and winked in my direction before turning back to the stove and stirring something that smelled delicious. Dad was dressed casually in a black Cozy Creek High School polo tucked into jeans. You couldn't really take the school out of the principal even on weekends.

"Anything I can do to help with dinner?"

"Would you mind setting the table?" he called absently over his shoulder.

"I can do that," I replied brightly, setting my glass on the counter.

While I didn't see Ginny's mystery boyfriend, I assumed he must be running late. Gathering up linen napkins, plates, and utensils for five, I headed to the adjacent dining room while Kimberly and Ginny continued their conversation, and my father monitored the saucepan.

I was straightening the last place setting when Ginny paused in the doorway to the dining room and said, "What are you doing?"

"Setting the table," I responded, ignoring her tone.

"There should only be four."

My head rose at Ginny's announcement. "Your boyfriend couldn't make it? I was looking forward to meeting him."

She crossed her arms defensively before curling her upper lip in a snarl. "He turned out to be a loser not worth my time."

"Oh, I'm sorry to hear that. Are you okay?"

Ginny's dark brows furrowed in confusion. "Of course I am."

I took in her crop top and wide-leg jeans, her full face of make-up, and her glossy brown hair with auburn highlights. She wasn't one of those horrible popular people who'd aged poorly since high school. Ginny was still beautiful—pretty packaging that she maintained ruthlessly.

"Well, I'm sure you'll meet someone else," I managed with some genuine sympathy. Dating was a bitch. I knew that first-hand. Ghosting and dick picks and the occasional married ass-hole trying to cheat on his wife had been my experience as I'd put an effort into online dating this past year. Heck, I'd even tried speed dating down at Bookers Pub and Grill. There hadn't been a single winner in the bunch and most never made it be-yond the first date.

An unladylike snort erupted out of my stepsister. "Are you try-ing to give *me* dating advice, Luanne?" Using my full name was her favorite. "I heard you got stood up last night at The Tavern. Don't worry, I'm sure you'll meet someone else," she repeated my words in a syrupy-sweet tone.

I held her dark gaze a moment before looking away in defeat. Inwardly, I cursed at another failed attempt to make anything of this relationship with Ginny. She was determined to keep up the spoiled princess routine, and I took a deep breath so I wouldn't snap out something nasty that I couldn't take back.

Gathering up the fifth place setting we wouldn't be needing, I avoided Ginny and went out the far end of the dining room and backtracked down the hallway into the kitchen.

Kimberly was now at the stove, and I spied my father manning the grill out on the deck. My stepmother wore what I called fancy loungewear. Her pale off-the-shoulder sweater looked soft and expensive, and her dyed-blond hair was piled high in a strategic-looking messy bun. Sparkling diamonds in her ears and a delicate gold link chain necklace around her neck completed the look.

She didn't turn as I approached. When I was done putting away all the unused dinnerware, I cleared my throat. Kimberly finally glanced over her shoulder in my direction.

I made sure my father's attention was still focused on the grill before speaking. "So, Kimberly, I wanted to talk to you about Dad's birthday coming up. I thought maybe we could plan a surprise party for him. Invite his friends from the racquet club and school, maybe his book club, too."

I could feel myself fighting to keep the smile on my face, my cheeks trembling at the edges as the silence stretched, and my stepmother looked at me with an awkward expression.

"Well, Ginny and I already made reservations at Laurel Park Inn for a nice dinner. It's your father's favorite, you know."

"Oh." Disappointment and confusion churned in my stomach as the smile I'd been trying to maintain fell away in heated embarrassment.

"You're more than welcome to join us," Kimberly rushed to add. "I can adjust the reservation."

"Thank you. That would be great." I nodded quickly to cover my hurt and the implications of her words. That I wasn't included in the first place. How I wasn't wanted. How everything involving my stepfamily was like pulling teeth.

Noah's matter-of-fact words floated back to me as I struggled through my feelings of frustration and anger. *"The effort of maintaining a relationship should go both ways and be equal. Not one person killing themselves to keep it all together."*

But then my dad entered the kitchen holding a platter of grilled chicken at the same time Ginny came to stand next to her mom. "There are my girls." He looked so happy as we all smiled back.

For as stilted and polite as my relationship with Kimberly had always been, she did seem to genuinely love my dad. After being married to Ginny's father—an aloof workaholic—for almost eighteen years, she was happy to have the attention of my soft-spoken and kind-hearted father—a man who made her a priority in ways her ex never had. Benjamin Billings had shown up to all my dance recitals and softball games. He'd attended my art shows and was an integral part of my life growing up. Kimberly saw his dedication and commitment and returned it with her own devotion and love. She might tolerate me, but she cared deeply for my father.

Even when I'd been grieving my mother and the life I'd once known—confused by my father's decision to marry so soon after her passing—I'd never tried to drive a wedge between my dad and Kimberly. I didn't understand it, but I was glad he'd found happiness again. If I had to put up with Kimberly's ambivalence, I would do it. And at some point during college, I decided that it wasn't enough to simply survive my new stepfamily. For my dad's sake, I wanted us to thrive.

My goals had changed after returning home to Cozy Creek. I'd gained confidence in art school and was excited to start my own business selling my artwork. I'd had time and distance from the horrors of high school and the lingering sadness of my hometown. I'd wanted to take the only family I had left and make it a family in truth. I craved togetherness—holidays and family dinners, celebrations and group chats. But we'd never really gotten there.

However, it didn't stop me from trying. Lu Billings was no quitter.

The meal progressed as usual, with Kimberly and Ginny dominating the conversation while Dad and I listened. I mentioned the Fall Festival next month to lay the groundwork on suggesting we all attend together. I'd bring it up again, but I needed to let them warm up to the idea. Maybe this was the year it would happen.

Dad asked, as he always did, about work while Ginny snorted pointedly. I ignored her and told him my online shop was doing well. Cozy Creek had a busy tourist season, so the farmers' market was pretty profitable for me since out-of-towners were interested in taking some inexpensive artwork home with them. Not to mention the greeting cards I made and the orders I'd need to fill before the upcoming holidays. Things were busy, but that was the way I liked it.

"You know there are some openings in the school district if you ever wanted to work with kids," Dad reminded me for possibly the thousandth time. "And I hear Shelby Hanzsek is retiring at the end of this school year."

Mrs. Hanzsek had been my elementary art teacher. I'd liked her a lot. She'd been a wonderful teacher, always encouraging me.

"You'd be great with kids, Lu," my dad said sincerely, pointing his fork in my direction. "And you'd get to use your art degree for something more than a hobby."

Ginny snorted again, and I glanced in her direction. "Sorry. Must be allergies or something."

My dad had resumed eating, but I still felt the need to say, "Yeah, I'll think about it."

A familiar discomfort settled in the pit of my stomach at the way my dad minimized my career. I knew how much he valued education and, of course, appreciated that he wanted the best for me. But it still stung that he didn't trust that I knew what was best for myself. Family gatherings went this way sometimes—

most times—but I tried to remember that my dad loved me. But with the nosedive in the conversation, I pretty much just moved the food around on my plate for the rest of the meal.

At four minutes until nine, I gathered my bag and told everyone good night, ignoring the way I only received two responses instead of three.

Noah and the Bronco waited in the driveway, the notes of a folk song I didn't recognize floating to me on the chilly night air. A smile spread across my face, and I hurried to the back seat.

"So how was it?" Noah said, tilting his head in my direction to pick up my answer.

I swallowed around the sore feeling and wistful regret that often lingered after a family dinner. "It was . . . fine," I finally settled on. I'd left my apartment with a hopeful heart and the best intentions for the evening. But over the course of the meal, I'd been reduced to something small and disappointed. I could feel the stiff ache in my shoulders from holding myself together so tightly. It was strange how encounters with my family could leave me feeling lonelier than ever.

Some twisted part of me didn't want to admit my struggles or acknowledge that Noah's words early in the evening had wrapped themselves around me and cast a shadow over every conversation with my family.

I could feel Noah's eyes on me in the rearview mirror as he put the vehicle in reverse. "Did the new boyfriend pass the test?"

"Oh," I replied, having nearly forgotten about the whole reason for the visit tonight. "He wasn't there. They broke up already.

Poor guy dodged a bullet." Then I immediately felt guilty for my snarky comment.

Noah laughed. "Was your stepsister upset?"

"Nah, not really."

"That's good."

Before silence could descend, I decided I wasn't ready to call it a night. I was in a weird mood from dinner and didn't want to let this loneliness fester. Eating my feelings felt like the way to go. And spending time with Noah had been the best part of my week so far. I wouldn't dwell too much on the way seeing his car idling in my father's driveway had given me a sense of relief. "Hey, want to grab some ice cream? I bet you haven't tried Dottie's yet. It's a hole-in-the-wall but makes the best waffle cones you've ever had in your life."

Noah stopped at a traffic light, and I could see the headlights behind him brighten his features in the mirror, showing his skeptical hazel eyes squint in my direction. "I don't know. What if your Best of Cozy Creek skills are limited to burgers and tots?"

Laughing, I replied, "Well, I guess you'll just have to take the leap and find out."

Despite the late hour, Dottie's parking lot was packed when we arrived.

I'd tried not to stare when Noah unfolded his tall, lean frame from the driver's seat of the Bronco and held the door open for me. But he was a good-looking guy. His light brown hair was a little messy again tonight, windblown and carelessly disheveled in a way that made me want to run my fingers through it.

He wore a tee shirt and jeans with the casual confidence of someone with a workout routine that involved cardio or an unfairly high metabolism. I'd forced myself to look away when Noah had shoved his hands in his front pockets and exposed a millimeter of toned midsection.

Once inside, I ordered a waffle cone with two scoops of pumpkin cheesecake swirl since it was quickly approaching my favorite season of the year. Noah opted for chocolate chip cookie dough, and I applauded his choice.

"Classic crowd-pleaser," I said after he'd given his order to the teenager behind the counter.

"I'm sorry, I didn't know I was being judged by my ice cream selection."

I gave him a slow blink and an expectant stare. "Of course. How else would I know if you were a serial killer?"

He paused in reaching for his wallet. "What would a serial killer order?"

Resisting the urge to crack up, I moved easily around him, inching closer to Kaitlyn working the cash register. "Pistachio. Obviously."

"God, I hate how much sense that just made."

I laughed, slipping my credit card to the Dottie's employee.

"You don't need to do that," Noah said sharply.

I spun to face him. "I invited you. It's my treat."

Dark brows furrowed over stormy eyes, Noah looked like he wanted to argue, but Kaitlyn was already swiping my card. And just then, the other employee got his attention to pass him his cone and mine.

"Thank you," Noah murmured quietly, but I noticed it took two attempts to swallow before he got the words out.

What could have happened to this guy that accepting an ice cream cone from someone felt like a concession? I wanted to hug him *and* buy him an ice cream. But I wouldn't. I'd give him some space instead.

I didn't say "you're welcome" or "anytime" or anything at all. I thought it might be better to pretend an exchange of goods and services had never occurred. So I snagged an empty table just as some tourists vacated the premises.

Part of me worried that Noah might not follow. That he might just take his cone and bail, but when I shimmied onto the bench of the small booth, Noah sat himself down on the seat across from me, knees bumping mine with every slide and adjustment.

Under the fluorescent lights of the establishment, Noah's skin looked like the sort of luminous pale that tanned easily in the summer, but maybe it had been a while since he'd seen the sun. I wondered again where he'd come from and why he'd relocated to Cozy Creek, but I knew better than to ask outright. Noah still wore his distrustful pants and, boy, were they cinched tight around the waist.

"So," I began, all nonchalance between licks of pumpkin cheesecake swirl, "how are you settling in to Cozy Creek life?

You're in an apartment above Main, right?" He'd mentioned it during our casual burger hang at Skytop. Leading with something proven safe felt like the right way to go.

Noah placed a napkin on his lap, and I resisted the urge to swoon over his table manners. My last blind date had talked with his mouth full, and I'd had to escape to the bathroom when a piece of tortilla chip had evacuated his mouth onto my cheek. I'd scrubbed my face with foaming hand soap and screamed into my palm.

"Yeah, I'm in one of the apartments above the Confectionery."

I noticed he ignored the first part. "Oh, nice. That place is great. Just don't get the coffee."

"What? Why?"

I grinned. "Just trust me on that."

We licked our ice cream for a few moments, comfortable quiet filling the space between us as an acoustic cover played through the speakers over our heads. I didn't let myself linger over watching Noah and his chocolate chip cookie dough. Friends didn't stare at their friends' tongues. Pretty sure that was a rule somewhere. And I was determined to be this guy's friend. Noah needed it. I could tell.

While I tried not to focus on his mouth, I kept an eye on his progress, waiting for him to get to his first bite of waffle cone. And yep. There it was.

Noah's eyes—swirling greenish-brown in this light—widened, then shot to mine. "Holy shit. This is amazing."

"I know, right?"

"Seriously. It's the best waffle cone I've ever had in my life. It's buttery and crisp. And, God, it's still warm."

"I'm two for two," I singsonged.

Noah eyed me over his cone, face relaxed for the first time since I'd paid for his treat. "You really are, Lulabelle."

I looked down to hide my smile at the nickname.

When I'd composed myself, I crunched into my own waffle cone, making sure to get a bite of pumpkin cheesecake swirl with it.

"We don't have ice cream cones like this back in South Carolina."

I stayed very still lest movement might startle the tight-lipped males of the species. "Oh yeah?" My tone was carefully casual.

"Yeah," Noah confirmed, his attention still fixed on the cone in his hand. "It's a really tiny town."

"I might know a thing or two about that."

He gave me a knowing grin. "Yeah, but Cozy Creek is full of tourists."

"Only certain months out of the year," I corrected.

"And fall is the big one, right?"

"Yep and winter for skiing and snowboarding, but that's mostly up at the resorts on the mountain. Tourists are already here in anticipation of all our fall events." I loved my town. Yes, Cozy Creek put on all these autumn spectacles to draw in visitors, but that didn't mean the residents couldn't enjoy them too.

While Noah devoured his cone bit by bit, I told him about what it was like to live in Cozy Creek. I broke down all the events from now through the huge New Year's Eve bash on Main Street to close out the year. He listened and asked questions about my favorite things to do. And when our knees bumped together under the table, he didn't shift and pull away.

When the ice cream was gone, I shared some of my experiences in college and told him about my two best friends, Emma and Cody. Noah returned the favor by talking about his life in Baxter, South Carolina, and his friends there.

Being with Noah was fun. I'd been able to forget why I'd invited him out for ice cream in the first place. I didn't think about the failed dinner across town or my family at all.

The whole night felt easy and comfortable, like when a song you used to love popped up randomly on shuffle. The words came effortlessly, and a warm weight settled over me—something remembered and soft around the edges from comfort and practice.

Maybe I needed this burgeoning friendship just as much as Noah did.

CHAPTER 3

Noah

The stellar ice cream hadn't been an anomaly. Turned out Lu Billings knew her stuff. And she also knew how to take nearly anything and make it fun.

It had been nice to talk about our hometowns without all the complicated feelings I had regarding both. She hadn't pushed on any of the topics of conversation, and as a result, I hadn't felt cornered and defensive.

Two days after our outing to Dottie's, I'd driven Lu to another first date before turning around and picking her back up twenty minutes later after her dinner companion took off during appetizers. He'd gone to the restroom and just never came back. Lu had gotten worried and messaged him through the dating app, but he'd already blocked her. She didn't seem too broken up about it. We'd gone for tacos at her favorite food truck in town instead. She'd shared some of her disaster dating stories from before I'd been her Huber driver, and I couldn't believe some of the douchebags she'd had to endure.

Just last night, her date had shown up with his mother. She'd made it through drinks at the bar before a text came in from Jimmy telling me to go back and get her. I'd had to pull over because we were laughing so hard while she recounted her time with the poor guy and his mom.

Then we'd hit a drive-through and parked in front of her building. We'd eaten chicken nuggets together and shared a large fry until a text from Jimmy told me to pick up someone who needed a ride to the Cozy Creek Lodge.

I knew whatever was going on between Lu and me was weird. It looked like friendship from the outside, but one dictated by her dating life and my job. I was skittish enough that she hadn't asked for my number so we could hang out together beyond her failed social engagements and my work schedule.

So far, she was content to be a friend to a guy who was obviously trying to keep his distance but was finding it increasingly difficult to resist her charms.

The problem wasn't with Lu. She was awesome—smart and funny and gorgeous and kind. We had a great time together and were friends, as quickly and unexpectedly as it had happened. I liked her a lot, but I didn't trust myself—not anymore.

Lu didn't put pressure on me by asking for more information than I was ready to give. I'd show up, call her a silly nickname to get her to smile, she'd guess something ridiculous about why I'd moved to Cozy Creek, and then we'd pick up where we left off the time before.

Despite the attraction I felt simmering beneath the surface, she'd never made a move on me. And there was no way I'd risk a new friendship with the only person in town I sort of knew.

I wasn't sure what I'd do when one of these first dates actually panned out for her. The thought of picking her up hours later and listening to her moon over someone else would be admittedly terrible.

But at least if she went home with the guy, I'd be spared the morning-after ride-share of shame. Henry would answer those requests since he was the Huber driver covering the day shift. Actually, that thought wasn't much better.

It was Friday afternoon and I'd just gotten my first text from Jimmy telling me to pick up Lu in the town square. I pulled up downtown to see a bunch of white booths set up around the gazebo. Circling the perimeter, I noticed firepits in the surrounding grass. Some people sat in clusters, gathered around with shopping bags and iced coffees, while the vendors under the tents seemed to be breaking down their displays and packing up their merchandise for the day. A large wooden sandwich board sign announced in hand-lettered script that this was the weekly farmers' market open on Fridays from June through October, specializing in flowers, produce, and handmade wares.

Lu stood on the sidewalk next to the loading zone with a huge shopping bag and three crates stacked neatly at her feet. Her ever-present oversized purse was on her shoulder, and I didn't know how she wasn't listing to the side. I'd seen her pull a bottle of wine from that thing before.

The boxes reached higher than her midsection, and she sipped a boba tea while waiting. Frowning, I stopped and shifted into park. Had she lugged all this stuff down from one of the booths herself?

I'd known that Lu had her own Etsy shop and made . . . things for customers. She'd mentioned it during that first night when we'd grabbed burgers together at Skytop Diner. But she hadn't elaborated.

"Heya, Noah." She smiled and bit her straw.

"Did you carry all this by yourself?" I demanded as I jumped out of the vehicle and went around to the back.

Her brows arched high on her forehead, and she lowered the plastic cup she held. "Um, yeah. I loaded up a little while ago before I called Jimmy to request a ride."

"How did you even get here with everything?"

"Henry brought me this morning and helped me to my booth." She tried for a reassuring smile. "Paused his audiobook and everything."

I hesitated to open the tailgate and looked at Lu. "Well, why didn't you—" I stopped myself from finishing that sentence. *Why didn't you call me and ask for help?*

Lu didn't even have my phone number. Our friendship wasn't like that. I was keeping everything safe and distant so I didn't fucking get hurt again.

Blowing out a breath, I pulled myself together. I was being ridiculous. She could manage on her own. Lu didn't need me.

She didn't say anything as she watched me lower the tailgate and step forward onto the curb to grab her things.

"Noah," she said softly, placing a staying hand on my forearm. Her skin was soft and warm, and she had a colorful beaded friendship bracelet that said "DeLuLu" on it. A delicate scent drifted over me—something warm and sweet that could dissolve on my tongue if given a chance. "Usually, I have my own car, and I set up and tear down and carry stuff all on my own. I have a cute little collapsible two-wheeler dolly and everything. Sometimes my best friend Cody comes and helps and sits with me in the booth. But I'm okay, I promise. I'm used to it."

I nodded without meeting her knowing gaze. Her hand fell away as I shifted the topmost crate into my arms and made for the back of the Bronco.

Together we got everything loaded and into the vehicle. Lu climbed in the back seat while I shifted a few crates to ensure they didn't topple over and spill their contents. One of the boxes had greeting cards on a display carousel in bright and eye-catching colors. Funny sayings and drawings were visible on the front of each piece of folded white cardstock. A brown envelope sat behind and accompanied the cards. I looked down in the next crate at matted and clear plastic-wrapped prints of varying sizes. The artwork was similar in style to the greeting cards, and the colors were, once again, vibrant and happy.

"These are awesome, Lucille Ball."

Lu turned to face me, propping her chin up on the seatback. She wore a grin and seemed to ignore my weirdness from before. "Thanks, beekeeper."

I smiled. "Why didn't you tell me you were an artist?"

She shifted a little in her seat. "I told you I had my own shop."

"Yeah, but not really what you did."

Lu sighed. "I don't know. People can be weird about it. Like it's this hobby I have."

Frowning, I asked, "But isn't it your job? Like, your only job, right? You don't work part-time somewhere else."

"No, this is my only form of employment. I'm not independently wealthy, but my online shop does well. I have a dedicated client base, and I supply greeting card stock to the General Store in town and other shops all over the country."

"That's amazing." I eyed her. Her gray eyes were shifty, and it was clear she wasn't super comfortable with the topic.

Closing the hatch and the tailgate, I climbed back in the driver's seat before spinning to face her. "Do you ever work on commissions for people?"

"Uh, no. Not anymore." She paused, and somehow, I knew to give her space with whatever she needed to work through. Lu finally offered, "I used to paint and draw a lot, but that's not really feasible to maintain unless original artwork is all I'm doing. I shifted my focus to what I'm doing now—premade digital art that I design myself and duplicate. It just made more sense from a business perspective."

I thought about what she'd said about people being weird

about her work and wondered who'd dimmed her light. "Do some people really consider this just a hobby and not a successful business that you own and operate like a badass art and design mogul?"

The smile was finally back on her face. "Mogul makes it sound like I'm an evil villain."

"Tycoon? Magnate? Lord of business? Chief of operations?" I offered instead.

"Boss babe extraordinaire, if you please."

Part of me wanted to let her divert. Probably the same part that was too much of a dumbass to give her my number and offer to carry her stuff.

Instead, I heard myself ask softly, "Who makes you feel like it's just a hobby, Lu?"

Her grin faded, and she held my gaze for a beat before admitting, "My family, I guess."

Ah, the same family she worked her ass off to keep together. One of our earliest conversations floated back to me—when I'd put my foot in my mouth and also put that kicked-puppy look on her face. The one she wore right now. It made my chest feel tight and uncomfortable to take someone like Lu—friendly and bright as the sun—and cast her in shadow.

"I'm sorry they make you feel like anything less than the boss babe extraordinaire you are."

"It's okay," she whispered. "Sometimes the people who've known you the longest have the hardest time seeing who you really are."

I nodded because that was so very true.

Facing forward, I started the Bronco and checked my mirrors before pulling away from the town square. "Do you think I can buy a print from you for my apartment? I could use some artwork in there."

"You know, there are a lot of amazing artists in the area. I bet you could find some really great artwork that you'd love."

"Are you saying you're too good to sell me one of your prints, Julia Louis-Dreyfus?"

She laughed in delight, a sound I loved to hear. "No, you weirdo. I'm saying there might be something better out there, more to your aesthetic. More your vibe."

I made the turn into the parking lot of Shady Peaks. "Maybe my vibe is colorful digital art. Maybe I'm a *live, laugh, love* sort of guy."

"Ha! Yeah, no way." Then she straightened in her seat. "Oh, that reminds me."

Instead of pulling up to the curb to let her out, I parked in a spot near her building, intent on helping her carry her things up. "Of what?"

"Why you moved here."

Unease had my hands tightening around the steering wheel. I knew Lu meant these little guesses all in good fun. There was no way she'd put together how I'd ended up in Cozy Creek. But every time she threw out some ridiculous scenario, I felt the reminder of the truth like a kick to the teeth.

Oblivious to my inner turmoil, Lu stated, "You moved here to attend Ms. Tammy's Cosmetology School, but sadly, you didn't pass the entrance exam of applying a perfect smoky eye and setting a perm."

I looked over my shoulder. "Ms. Tammy would be lucky to have me."

She cackled before grabbing her sinkhole of a purse and hopping down from the SUV. "You don't have to help me carry all this up."

I shot her a look as I joined her by the tailgate. "Right."

"I'm just saying! I can manage."

"I know. You're a boss babe extraordinaire. And now you get to boss me around for ten minutes while I pack mule your wares to your door."

She cringed, her nose crinkling adorably. "Don't say wares. It makes them sound like sex toys."

I choked out a laugh.

It took two trips for us to manage all her things, riding the elevator up to the fourth floor each time.

Lu unlocked the door to her apartment and shuffle-kicked-dragged one of the crates inside as she held the door for me and simultaneously flipped on the light switch. Her apartment was exactly how I imagined. It was inviting and comfortable with bright splashes of color. A midnight-blue velvet couch dominated the living room. It was wide and deep with a mountain of throw pillows spanning every color in the rainbow.

An amazing wooden sculpture drew my eye to the large wall spanning the length of the main room. The light-colored wood twisted and flowed into branches like a tree from where it perched on the shelf.

Lu saw me eyeing the piece. "It's custom. By this fantastic artist Levi Carmichael. He's ridiculously talented, and he gave me the local pricing. You should check him out. You're a local now."

"Yeah, maybe I will," I agreed. "It's amazing."

She beamed. "Here, let me take that." She snatched the box I'd been holding and moved through the living room, past the open-concept kitchen, and down the hallway, calling over her shoulder, "I use the second bedroom as an office and store all this stuff in there."

I took a moment to grab everything else we'd left in the hallway and brought it inside. Feeling weird about following her deeper into the apartment, I stood there awkwardly.

Lu returned. Amusement radiated from her, as if my discomfort and hesitancy in her home were entertaining. "You can just leave those there. I'll grab them later."

"Oh, okay," I said, taking a few steps back.

"Do you want to stay? I can order a pizza. Turn on a movie." She paused, unaware of how my heart pounded out a violent rhythm in my chest at her innocent invitation. "I just realized, I have no idea what sort of movies or shows you watch. How have we not discussed this? What if you're a *Star Trek* person and not a *Star Wars* person?"

I was actually a *Doctor Who* person.

"I should probably get going," I said instead. "I'm still on shift."

The excuse fell pretty flat. We'd hung out several times in the past couple of weeks while I was working—I just kept my phone with me and left if a ride request came in. So far, it hadn't been an issue or problem.

If Lu was upset by my quick rejection, she didn't show it. She smiled and said, "Okay. Well, I really appreciate your help carrying all my stuff up."

I took another step back, closer to the front door—needing space, needing room to breathe through my own fucking hangups and the disappointment twisting through me at what I was doing. I wanted to stay. I wanted to eat pizza and watch a movie on that blue couch surrounded by a Skittles-color array of throw pillows.

But I couldn't.

"Here, let me grab the money for my ride." She scrambled for her bag and started digging through it.

"It's okay," I heard myself say, desperate to flee.

Unaware of my inner turmoil, Lu didn't look up. She kept digging through her cavernous purse for cash and said, "No, don't be silly."

Retreat was the only thing on my mind. I'd just turned away and closed my fist around the doorknob when Lu's small hand landed on my forearm, stalling my escape.

I was unsteady already, and the feel of her soft, warm hand on my arm was doing unholy things to my balance. I'd been so careful to keep my distance and avoid casual touches with her. But Lu was pressing bills carefully into my other hand and closing my stiff fingers around them. It was all so innocent and over in the space of a breath. But in that single exhalation, my mind spun in circles, landing on a million complications over and over again.

"Thanks again." Her words were soft but they echoed loudly in my head.

"No problem," I mumbled, meeting her gray gaze that was far too knowing. She was so close I could smell that warm, sweet scent again—something vanilla and spice that lived on her skin and in her hair. The blond waves were loose and misbehaving, wild around her pretty face.

She saw me looking and tucked a strand behind her ear. "See you around, Noah."

I shoved my hand—and her money—in my pocket before I could do something stupid like run my fingers through her hair.

"Bye, Lu," I breathed into the charged atmosphere between us.

And then I bolted, sucking in the fresh fall evening air, attempting to get the scent of her out of my lungs and out of my head.

A tiny voice that sounded suspiciously like self-awareness whispered through the mountains that it was already too late.

CHAPTER 4

Cody: Hug Emma's neck for me

Me: I willllll

Cody: Have fun with Noah Sad Boy

Cody: Enjoy that looooong ride to Denver

Me: Are you done?

Cody: One more

Cody: Don't let that back seat go to waste

Cody: Okay, I'm done.

Me: See you when I get back. Don't forget me on Thursday.

Shaking my head, I fought a smile and took a sip of my pumpkin-spiced coffee. My best friend was ridiculous.

The mid-September sun was bright overhead, and I pulled off the hoodie I'd been wearing all morning while working on my tiny back deck that faced the mountains.

The leaves on the trees at the base of the Rockies were starting to change. Bright yellows, bold ochers, and deep reds emerged beautifully. I took a deep breath and reveled in my favorite time of year.

My mom had loved autumn most of all, so maybe that was why it was so special to me. I baked snickerdoodles in the fall months and thought of her. I remembered painting pumpkins and walking the corn maze together—doing the cheesy tourist things that brought her so much joy.

This time of year was when my memories of her were the strongest and brightest, filling me up and squeezing my heart just shy of breaking.

I turned my attention back to the watercolor paper in front of me and smiled. I was working on something for Noah—a piece I planned to matte to go in his apartment. I fought the urge to laugh. He was going to love it.

It had been a long time since I broke out my watercolors. Typically, all the work I did for my shop was digital. But it felt good to stretch my creative legs this morning and dip my toes back in the water, so to speak. Creating original artwork was something I used to love. From painting at the kitchen table with my art-loving mother to visiting museums on every family vacation, that part of my life was special.

My background was in studio art as well as graphic design, but pursuing painting and drawing hadn't been realistic, according to my dad. He was right about it being more time-consuming and less reliably profitable. I didn't have a dedicated studio space or any connections to galleries. It was smarter and safer to keep doing what I was doing. I wanted to be successful in business, not just for myself. I wanted my father to see the work I put into my profession, but that hadn't been the case so far.

I ignored the shallow ache I felt when I thought about letting the creative side of me go dormant. But business owners had to make tough decisions. Maybe moving forward, I could occasionally get out my watercolors or charcoal just for me—not for profit. Paint and draw for fun like I used to as a kid before I decided that art was my path. Before I made it a career.

I liked my work with DeLuLu Designs. Yet it had been nice to work on something original for Noah—something special that couldn't be reproduced and sold to someone else at the farmers' market. He wouldn't understand the significance, but it was probably better that way. It would likely scare him off for good.

I could rush and finish the painting today to give to him, but I needed to pack and prep everything for my flight tonight. I was visiting my friend Emma in New Mexico for a quick four-day trip that we'd arranged a few months prior. Earlier in the day, I'd called Jimmy and arranged for Noah to drive me to the airport at 6:00 p.m. sharp.

Yes, it was probably stupid to have booked an evening flight just so Noah could be the one to take me to Denver. But I liked spending time with him and didn't want to put Cody out by asking for a favor. Over an hour's drive to the airport would mean that my BFF would need to request off from work, and I didn't want to make his life harder. Plus, he thought whatever was going on with Noah needed to evolve into "sexy, fun times" since we were both so "adorably smitten with each other." Cody hadn't met Noah yet, but I could only keep him away for so long. And he'd heard me talking about the Huber driver enough to sit up and take notice.

I'd only started online dating at my friend's encouragement anyway. He thought it was hilarious that I was falling for the guy driving me to all my first dates instead.

I rolled my eyes at that ridiculous assumption. I barely knew Noah. Yes, we were friendly, but sometimes it seemed like that was entirely against his will. And of course I was attracted to him. Noah was gorgeous—all grumpy and scowly with that messy brown hair, the permanent scruff on his jaw, and those amazing hazel eyes. We had fun together. He was easy to talk to and so clever and funny. His sarcastic quips usually had me doubled over, while his dry delivery didn't even make his mouth twitch.

We were . . . friends. And I wanted to spend time with him. So far, requesting a ride had been the only safe way to do that. I didn't want to put too much pressure on him and scare him off—like how he'd practically sprinted out of my apartment two days ago. Hence the Huber request to the Denver International Airport.

It was probably pretty pathetic and reflective of my failed dating life that I paid a guy to hang out with me. Oh God. Was this prostitution? Was that only if sex was involved?

I set the paintbrush aside and swiped a palm down my face. Shit, I was a mess.

Four hours later, I was packed and waiting on the sidewalk in front of my building with a bright purple carry-on when Noah pulled up in the Bronco.

His window was down, and he had one toned forearm resting on the doorframe. "Get in, Lu-ser. We're going to the airport."

My mouth dropped open, and I stared at him incredulously. "Did . . . did you just quote *Mean Girls*?"

Noah climbed out of the SUV and reached for my bag. "I don't know what you're talking about," he replied, dry as dirt, but his hazel eyes sparkled.

"Oh my God!" I cracked up.

Noah got my luggage secured while I climbed in the back seat. Part of me thought about testing the limits and hopping in the front, but I knew that probably wasn't wise. Besides, if Noah really wanted me to sit up there with him, he would have moved his little travel cooler.

"So where are you going?" Noah asked as he settled himself behind the steering wheel. "You didn't mention a trip."

I guess we weren't addressing the awkward way he'd bolted from my apartment the other night.

"Just down to Albuquerque for a few days to visit my friend Emma. We went to college together. You know the Cody I've mentioned? Well, the three of us met at Western Colorado. Cody moved to Cozy Creek after college, but Emma got married and lives in New Mexico with her husband. Our schedules lined up, so I decided to take a quick trip. I'll have a ton of cards to prep before the holiday rush coming up, so if I don't go now, I won't get a chance."

"Gotcha," Noah replied to my long-winded history lesson. "When are you coming back?"

My instinct was to tease him and ask if he'd miss me. Instead, I went the cautious route and answered, "I'll be back Thursday, but don't worry. Cody will pick me up so you don't have to hoof it all the way to Denver to come get me."

Noah's gaze met mine briefly in the rearview mirror before he turned his attention back to the road and merged onto Highway 62.

I took a breath and said, "You'll get a break from me for a few days. That should be nice." I threw in a chuckle so I didn't sound quite as pathetic as I felt.

The silence stretched, and embarrassment had me shifting in my seat. Noah didn't say he'd be glad for the breathing room. He also didn't say he'd miss hanging out. Nor did he ask for my number so we could text while I was away. He just did this little laugh in the front seat that was more breath than anything else.

I was a strong, independent woman. I could ask Noah for his number—even as friends. I texted my friends all the time. That wasn't anything unusual. But, again, my thoughts drifted back to Friday in my apartment. The mere thought of pizza and a movie in my living room had him giving Olympic sprinters a run for their money. I'd gotten too close, too familiar. Asking for his number might have him dumping me on the side of the road and hightailing it back to Cozy Creek without me.

What could have happened to Noah to make him so skittish? A bad breakup, maybe. Did someone cheat on him? Maybe he was grieving a loss.

Noah would tell me when he was ready. Despite how much I liked him and how attracted I was, I could control it. If friendship was all Noah wanted, then that was okay.

It would have to be.

"So you're not missing family dinner tonight?" Noah's question jolted me out of my thoughts.

I cleared my throat. "No, we don't have them on a schedule or anything. Plus it's a pretty busy time right now for Cozy Creek High. Dad is the principal there. The students and the staff are preparing for the Fall Carnival fundraiser and the Fall Ball. My stepmother, Kimberly, is the chair of the parent-teacher organization and oversees the decorations and chaperones and all that stuff. But we do have my dad's birthday dinner coming up in a few weeks, so that should be fun."

Despite the disappointment surrounding that lack of dinner invitation, I was determined to make it a fun occasion for my dad.

"What was it like having your dad as your principal?"

"Oh." I paused, thinking. "I guess we didn't overlap much, honestly. He used to give me rides to school before I had my own car, but then we usually went our separate ways. I was never the sort of kid who broke the rules and needed to call in favors to get me out of trouble." That was more Ginny's thing. Senior year, she'd gotten caught vaping in class.

"Really?" Noah said, grinning. "You were a goody-goody? I figured you'd be prom queen, head cheerleader, and all-around troublemaker."

"What? No. I was an art nerd. I played softball until tenth grade, and Latin was my favorite class. I wasn't unpopular or anything. I had my group of friends who were all pretty good kids, and we just survived high school together, I guess."

"I can see that, too."

The sun was already behind the mountains, and the shadows were growing longer. The interior of the Bronco was getting dim, and I couldn't make out Noah's expressions as easily until the headlights from a passing car illuminated his face.

Wondering if this was a safe topic, I ventured, "What were you like in high school?"

"Busy, mostly," he replied. "I played soccer in the fall and ran track in the spring."

"Oh, cool. Do you still run?"

"Yeah, usually after I wake up, I do a few miles around town first thing. It took me a minute to adjust to the altitude, but I'm almost up to speed now. Why, do you want to be my running partner?"

I laughed. "Yeah, no. I don't do that. But I appreciate the vote of confidence. If you ever decide to try rock climbing, I'm your girl." I considered briefly, not wanting to stick my nose where it didn't belong, but then I just went for it. "One of my friends from high school actually, runs daily around town. Have you met Cole Sutter?"

At the shake of Noah's head in the negative, I continued, "He's part of the Cozy Creek Fire Brigade. A really nice guy. And he runs in all the local races. I could introduce you if you wanted. I think running is about as fun as a dental cleaning, but I'm sure it would be better to have a friend to do it with."

If Noah had more friends in town, maybe he'd be more settled. Sometimes it seemed like he was one strong breeze from blowing away. Like he chose driving for Jimmy so he could always be ready to roll out of town at a moment's notice.

"Yeah, maybe. Music or podcast?" Noah called suddenly, signaling the end of that conversation.

I ignored the twinge of disappointment I felt. "Music, if it's upbeat. Podcast, if it's murdery."

He laughed, even, white teeth flashing in the rearview. "Why am I not surprised?" he said, but he was still smiling. "Here. Pick something, Luna Lovegood."

While I'd been staring at him in the mirror like a lovestruck groupie, he'd tossed his cell phone in my lap with his music app open. I scrolled for a few minutes until I found an album I'd been obsessed with lately.

When the opening sounds of guitar strings filled the Bronco,

Noah's eyes flew to mine in the rearview mirror. "I thought you said upbeat?"

"Most of the album is upbeat," I argued. "I don't care. I love it."

"Me too," he admitted.

"Then turn it up, beekeeper."

He did. And for the next hour, we belted out lyrics. I was louder than he was, but we had fun with it. We sang about dialing drunk and being homesick. Music filled the Bronco and carried us all the way to Denver. It made us shout our favorite parts and nod our heads in time together. And when the final song ended, I felt breathless. Linked with Noah through this shared experience. Like I'd never be able to listen to this album again without thinking of him.

The more time we spent together, the bigger our friendship felt. It was the ease with which we spoke. The way he listened when I talked and didn't seem to mind when we disagreed.

Making friends as an adult was hard. My friends from high school were people I'd known all my life. They knew my stories, and I knew where they came from. College was my first chance to really go out and choose who I surrounded myself with. There was a little catching up with Emma and Cody, but eventually, I'd learned about their pasts and what made them the young adults they were. But we had the college experience to solidify our connection. Late nights and parties, studying and inside jokes. Our lives merged in a way that felt like forever.

Outside of an education setting, most adult friendships were formed through employment and forced proximity. Those experiences bonded. I worked from home and didn't really have an avenue to meet new people. Tourists came and went in Cozy Creek, but it had been a long time since I'd made a new friend from scratch, so to speak.

Noah had so much history—twenty-seven years of it—that I didn't know. But with every ride, I wanted to know more. I wanted to hear all his secrets and soak up every bit of Noah Cooper I could.

For me, the idea of learning all the ins and outs of his life was exciting. I looked forward to it. But for Noah, I could tell he wanted to keep the past in the past. He was guarded, withholding to protect himself, and it made me sad to know that someone had given him a reason to be so cautious. I had marks against me before we'd even met.

Like magic, the car went quiet as Noah took the exit to the airport. I told him my airline and terminal, and we made the remainder of the drive in comfortable silence. Well, mostly comfortable. My skin was buzzing pleasantly from the last hour we'd spent together.

I dropped the cash for the trip on the center console as Noah hopped out to grab my luggage. We met on the curb as traffic jerked and halted around us in the loading zone, streetlights casting everything in an otherworldly orange glow.

"There's no way that purse is making it on the plane," he said, eyeing my bag.

Giving him my best mock scowl, I hoisted my bag higher on my shoulder. "I'll have you know that this counts as a personal item."

Noah snorted. "Hope you took your wine bottle out."

I whacked him on the shoulder, and he laughed.

"Good luck in town while I'm gone. You should be able to focus on the task that brought you there."

He raised one dark brow expectantly. "Which is?"

"Cozy Creek has the largest population of slugs in North America. You moved here to study them."

"Ew. What? No." He looked horrified. "Is that true?" He looked down at the concrete like a slug might jump out and attack him.

"Calm down, nerd. You're in Denver, and you're standing on a street. Pretty sure you're safe. Also, I totally made that up."

Noah's glare was baleful, but his hazel eyes were bright with amusement.

With a tiny step forward, the toes of my polka-dot ballet flats were right on the edge of the sidewalk. Noah stood just below me on the street. The step up put us at eye level, and I decided to be brave.

"Can I have a hug before I go?"

He looked hesitant, hands tucked firmly in the pockets of his jeans.

Despite him being in town for over a month, I thought I might be his only friend in Cozy Creek so far. I knew I needed to play this cool, but I wanted him to know, in some small way, that I would miss him and be thinking of him. And part of me thought he might need this hug more than I did. Noah was so averse to connections, unwilling or unable to rely on anyone or trust their good intentions. I didn't mind his cynical nature, but I did worry about how his self-imposed detachment might affect him in the long run.

Just when I thought he might refuse my request, Noah straightened and removed his hands from his pockets.

Just to make absolutely sure, I added, "It's just that, if I die on that plane . . . "

"Oh my God," he groaned, rolling his eyes.

I smiled and then sobered to repeat dramatically, "If I die on that plane, I'd really like a hug before I go."

"Come here, you absolute corn nut." He reached out and snagged me about the waist. Noah pulled me in close and propped his chin on my shoulder while I wrapped my arms around his neck.

He smelled sweet like the yellow Starburst he kept in his cup holder, and his body was warm beneath his blue tee shirt despite the chill in the autumn air. I let myself squeeze him tight for six and a half seconds before I made myself pull away.

Noah was still smiling. "Have a safe flight, Lunar Lander. I'll see you when you get back."

"Thanks, Noah." I grinned. "See you."

He stayed right there on the street, hands tucked in the pockets of his dark-wash jeans while I wheeled my bag into the airport terminal. I gave him a wave before I walked through the automatic doors and hoped my expression wasn't as dreamy and wistful as it felt.

Noah's face was solemn again, the amusement from our conversation now just a memory shadowing his features. He raised his hand in return as I disappeared inside.

As I made my way to the security checkpoint, I worried that if I was out of sight and out of mind, what would Noah be like when I returned to Cozy Creek later this week? If I wasn't there to make the effort, would our friendship die in the beginning stages?

I didn't know how to show Noah he was safe with me. That I would defend his heart and keep it safe. I'd have his back. Because that was what friends did for one another.

And if a tiny part of me hoped to do more than safeguard his heart, I'd just have to keep reminding myself that Noah wasn't mine to keep.

CHAPTER 5

Noah

I didn't know why, but this week seemed extra long. As a reluctant resident of Cozy Creek, I admittedly didn't have much of a life. Maybe that was why.

Making friends hadn't been at the top of my to-do list since moving to town. Especially now that I didn't plan on staying. It seemed like a wasted effort. I knew my boss, Jimmy, of course. I was friendly with the staff at the Cozy Creek Confectionery and the coffee shop because, outside of the Bronco and my apartment, that was where I visited most often.

And then there was Lu, who caught me off guard and sneaked past my defenses. She was my . . . friend. Sure, a friend I found funny and smart and smoking hot. But she was just a friendly person.

Lu was knee-deep in everything Cozy Creek. She seemed like the sort of individual who asked after her mail carrier's grandkids or led a book club once a month. She probably volunteered for committees or helped out at the local animal shelter. Her giving and charitable nature was likely why she made such an effort with me. My one-woman welcoming committee. She destroyed my walls, one brick at a time, and shredded my careful self-control despite my best efforts. She would definitely hate the fact that I was just sort of floating through my existence here in Colorado.

Most mornings, I went for a run and stopped in the bakery downstairs for a meal. The rest of my time was spent working. My free time went toward building my new website and job hunting. The search for new employment was pretty open-ended. I was willing to work from home or move anywhere in the continental United States as soon as I had enough money saved. But I didn't think I would have much luck finding work in my field. Potential employers tended to review past job experience. There was no way in hell that anything from my previous employer would lend itself in my favor.

As a result, plan B was in the works. I'd gone to college for computer science, but strayed from my chosen field of web and app design when I'd landed a job in my hometown. The local grocery chain had offered on-the-job training for a help desk position, and honestly, employment was limited where I was from. As a twenty-year-old college student, I hadn't been ready to uproot and branch out. Smith Foods hired me part-time my senior year, and once I graduated, I stepped right into a full-time role. I wasn't doing web design, but I was still in the tech field and making decent money with room for advancement. So I'd stuck with it for seven years and was the help desk manager when all was said and done. Smith Foods had been my first and only real job.

Now that decision was biting me in the ass.

I hadn't landed a single interview or any recruiter interest, and the reason was my own damn fault.

Sighing, I glanced up from my laptop. The apartment came furnished. Thank you very much, Landlord Gigi, because I didn't have much. My computer, some clothes, a box of books, and a handful of other mementos were the only things that survived the great purge and made the trip with me out West.

The furniture was all fine—comfortable and lived in. But nothing here was anything I would have picked for myself. The throw pillows were all subdued, not like the rainbow of accessories over at Lu's place. The walls were mostly bare, and, again, I thought of buying something from her shop—something to make this place more mine.

But what was the point of that? I didn't think I could stay here in Cozy Creek. In fact, plan B hinged on me leaving this town.

Ignoring the blank gray walls, I brushed away thoughts of Lu while I was at it. Safer that way. Then I checked the time in the corner of my screen. 2:48 p.m. I had time to hit the grocery store for some things I needed before my Huber shift started at five.

The General Store wasn't far. It didn't have all the essentials, but I could get by for a while until I needed to travel outside of town to go to a Wal-Mart or Target.

Grabbing a basket on my way in, I gave a nod to the cashier who greeted me. I was pretty sure her name was Betsy. A few people were wandering through the aisles. I could pick out the tourists, for the most part, by their plaid scarves and general air of "look how cute this tiny store is!" as they gawked and pointed.

I'd just hit the snack aisle when I spotted Lu along the back wall of the store reaching for a bottle of wine. Her back was to me, and I stood frozen for a second as I watched her rise onto the toes of her leopard-print ballet flats, her petite form straining for a bottle on the top shelf. Her blond hair cascaded down her back in unruly waves. I could see a headband peeking out among the strands. She wore dark tights under an emerald-green skirt. Her peacoat and ridiculous purse hid everything else.

An unexpected smile lit my features as I took her in. Relief and joy had me feeling like a middle schooler with a crush. I'd missed this girl. Missed her conversation and our car rides. Her constant need to feed me and her questionable taste in music. I'd missed her red lips and her smiles aimed right at me.

And with that awareness came a cold sense of dread followed closely by utter fucking panic.

I suddenly realized why this week had seemed to drag on endlessly. I hadn't seen Lu since I'd dropped her at the airport four days ago. Since she'd hugged me goodbye like I was someone she'd known her whole life . . . someone who was a real friend . . . like I was *someone* period. She felt so good in my arms, but I'd forced myself to step back and let her go.

All of these complicated and conflicting thoughts flitted through my mind while I stood there like an idiot.

Lu dropped back onto her heels with a dull click, wine bottle in hand, and I panicked. I darted around the corner of the aisle and flattened myself against an endcap of potato chips.

Why was I hiding from her? This was insane. I could just go say hi or offer to help her get more wine down from the top shelf. But my feet wouldn't move.

I was breathing harder than I should have been, thinking through scenarios. Lu would smile when she saw me. She always did. It made me feel like she'd flicked that sunlamp on again in the center of my chest. What if she wanted to hug me again? Maybe that would be a hello thing as well as a goodbye thing since I'd let it happen the last time.

Footsteps sounded coming toward me. I stopped trying to predict the future and instead worried about the present. She must be walking up the aisle I'd just vacated.

I took my basket and bolted down the next row, careful to keep my back facing the front of the store. I could feel myself losing control of the situation. I didn't know why seeing Lu in this context—no Huber request in the vicinity—was freaking me out, but the very possibility of running into her unexpectedly was causing pressure to build in my chest.

My anxious steps carried me to the end of the aisle facing the wall of wine bottles once more. But from the corner of my eye, I saw Lu still standing there. *Shit*. That must have been someone else I heard walking in the other direction because my pint-sized nightmare remained there, considering the meager selection of pinot noir.

I spun around as quickly as I could, almost clipping the endcap in the process but I saw Lu turn at the movement. I made for the exit, returning the way I'd just come, ignoring the flash of surprise I'd seen along with wide gray eyes.

"Noah?" Lu's voice came from behind me.

I nearly froze, but instead, I kept walking. She didn't call out again, and when I dropped my basket in the stack by the front door, I exhaled a desperate breath. Only relief didn't come. My chest remained tight with panic, and now a layer of shame coated me in a second skin.

Why the hell had I run away from Lu?

Outside the General Store, the afternoon was mild and comfortable. The sky clear and blue behind the mountains. It was all so at odds with the turbulence I felt within.

As I walked back to my apartment, I nearly stepped off the sidewalk into the path of a cyclist. I was distracted and hated myself. I had just pretended she wasn't there because I didn't want to face her. Because maybe I cared about this girl who was practically a stranger. Because I'd missed her while she was gone and had thought about that hug more than I wanted to admit.

The surprise in the store had done something to my brain. Seeing Lu outside of the Bronco and the confines of my carefully structured life had made her . . . real. More than just someone I saw at work. More than all the things I was trying to keep separate. More than an idiot guy with a crush on his fare. More than the connection I'd been trying to ignore. Seeing her in real life took all those mores and made them true.

And I was an asshole.

She'd seen me, and I'd ignored her. I'd walked right out that door, too scared to trust myself. Too panicked over feeling anything real for anyone ever again.

It didn't take me long to figure out how to fix what I'd done regarding Lu. But I had to wait until the following day to put my plan into action.

I happened to have Friday off this week while Jimmy covered my shift. Checking the hours of operation for the farmers' market, I waited until four o'clock and then hopped in the Bronco.

I wasn't sure which booth was Lu's, but I entered the town square near where I'd picked her up last week. Foot traffic had slowed this late in the afternoon, but I still kept a vigilant watch for anyone I didn't want to run into.

Most of the people looking for autumn produce had come and gone, picking through the baskets of fresh apples and squash. Only a few of the fall bouquets remained at the florist's tent, but the vendors still greeted customers as people looked over their jewelry or handknits or canned goods.

Finally, I walked through the gazebo in the center of the space and spotted Lu in her booth. A colorful sign hung behind her head at the back of the tent. DeLuLu Designs was written in bold script, flirty and fun—just like the boss babe behind the work. The greeting card carousel was on one end of the table, while the prints were displayed on the other.

Lu was smiling and talking to two teenage girls. I hung back and waited while she bagged up their purchases and accepted their payments.

She wore the beaded friendship bracelets again, and I saw several for sale on her table as well. Her lips were that distracting shade of fire-engine red, and the wild blond hair I was obsessed with was tamed with a striped black headband with a little knot at the top.

Lu caught sight of me lingering in front of her booth as she told the two customers goodbye. Her eyes widened a little when she spotted me, but then her focus returned to the teenagers.

Maybe I'd been so fixated on gauging her reaction that no one else would have caught it. The surprise had been there and gone so fast that I almost missed the tiny wince of hurt that accompanied it.

I swallowed hard against the shame swirling in my stomach.

The two girls finally stepped away from the booth, and I approached.

Lu made a big show of looking behind me, and my guilt climbed higher into my throat. Was she going to bring up what had happened at the General Store? Was she planning on ignoring me the way I'd snubbed her?

"Hi," I managed amid some awkward throat-clearing.

Her expectant gaze found mine. "There's no Bronco attached

to you. So weird."

I huffed a surprised laugh.

Lu wore a genuine grin as she watched me stand there with my hands stuffed in the pockets of my jeans. I hung on to that smile like a buoy in a storm—like a lifeline. It was forgiveness I didn't deserve.

"I was planning on calling a Huber later when I finished here. How fortuitous that you should arrive just before closing."

"Actually, it's my day off," I admitted.

"Oh." She suddenly looked embarrassed, cheeks going instantly pink as she backpedaled. "I'm so sorry. I shouldn't have assumed."

"No," I said quickly to reassure her. "I came to see you. I wanted to get a print for my apartment. I thought if I came later in the day, I wouldn't bother you as much. And that maybe I could help you pack up and take you home."

"Oh," she repeated. The humiliated expression was slow to leave as something thoughtful settled in its place.

"That sounds good, Noah." Before I could analyze her answer or worry about how my invitation might be received, she continued, "I'm really glad you came by. I actually made something for you. For your apartment."

The smile stretched across my face before I could stop it. "For me?"

"Yep," she replied, already rummaging around in a crate beneath the table. "But you can't look at it yet. Wait until you get home."

Lu produced a flat brown paper bag with DeLuLu Designs stamped across the front. I ran my hand across the logo.

My grin turned suspicious. "Thanks. What do I owe you?"

"Nothing," she said, waving off my attempts to hand her money from my wallet. "It's a housewarming gift. Welcome to Cozy Creek and all that. Plus, my friends get free art."

"Should my friends get free rides?" I countered, tucking the package carefully under my arm and refusing to acknowledge how warm her gift made me feel.

"Hell, no," Lu said. "I'm terrified of Jimmy. I don't want him to kill me."

I laughed.

She stood suddenly and started gathering her things. "It's close enough to closing time. Come on. We can pack up, and then I'll take you to the bubble tea truck. Did you get a chance to look at the other vendors?"

"Not really. Just in passing."

"Okay, cool. I'll take you around. There's a good turnout today."

For reasons I didn't want to identify too closely, I was reluctant to admit to Lu that it was pointless for me to get *more* settled in Cozy Creek. I didn't need to meet people or check out local vendors if I was leaving when the opportunity arose. The thought of telling her seemed wrong. She loved this town, and I knew she wouldn't understand that someone might want to leave. Disappointing her was the last thing I wanted to do. I'd already done that enough with my erratic, unhinged behavior.

Plus, I was here to make up for the way I'd acted at the General Store, and I couldn't bring myself to dim her light by being an asshole again. I didn't want to say no anyway. I liked spending time with her, as stupid and misguided as that was. And if she wanted to take me around, then I would go.

"That would be great. Thanks, Louie Anderson."

Her answering smile was a thing of beauty.

Forcing myself to look away from those tempting red lips, I gathered the greeting cards from the rack in front of me, following Lu's lead as she packed away her merchandise. "How was your trip to New Mexico?"

"It was great. We went to Santa Fe and walked around downtown, visited the St. Francis Cathedral. Had amazing food." She paused with a handful of stickers in her grasp. "It was good for the soul, you know? Sometimes you just need to see your friends, and a video call won't cut it."

I nodded, thinking about my friends back in South Carolina. They probably thought I'd dropped off the face of the planet.

"But I was ready to be home, too. I love fall. It's my absolute favorite. I like going to all the town events—which you should really check out, by the way."

"Yeah," I agreed and passed her some prints to pack in her crates.

"Thanks for offering to take me home. On your day off and everything."

"It's no trouble. That's what friends are for," I said, the reminder feeling necessary and tasting like ash on my tongue. "You're probably eager to get your car back. How long has it been now?"

"Oh," she mumbled, reaching beneath the table to grab something. "A few weeks."

"It must have really been busted. Was it bodywork or engine work? You weren't in an accident or anything, were you?"

"No accident," she called, still busy under the table. "They're fixing something with the carburetor . . . um, shaft . . . tank."

I eyed her. Pretty sure a carburetor shaft tank wasn't a real thing, but whatever.

"Okay! All packed up!" Her cheeks were pink when she finally emerged from digging beneath the table. "Let's go look around."

Lu led me down the main aisle toward a small trailer. The sign next to the open window said Aunt Pearl's Tea Palace. I met Amari, who owned Lu's favorite beverage shop in town. The middle-aged woman was delighted to see us, especially when I asked her to make me her favorite. She bragged sweetly on Lu, whispering conspiratorially that she was the one responsible for the hand-painted sign on the side of the trailer. She'd also helped Amari with branding and marketing materials.

I slid a glance to see Lu fidgeting with her bag and avoiding the attention.

After that we ventured around to the remaining vendors. Lu introduced me to the people she knew—nearly all of the ones we passed—and had me smelling hand-poured candles and goat's milk soap and trying samples from someone selling shortbread cookies. We walked and talked and sipped our teas for half an hour before returning to Lu's table.

"You ready, pack mule?"

"Just about," I replied, pulling out my phone. I resisted the nervous desire to shove it in my pocket and forget this dumb idea. But I needed to try harder and be better where Lu was concerned. The incident at the General Store was proof of that. I could be a better friend to the girl who'd done nothing but try her best to befriend me. "Do you want to exchange numbers? That way, you don't have to call Jimmy to reach me. And I could help you carry your stuff." I could see the argument gathering on her features, so I rushed to add, "Even though I know you're used to doing it yourself, and you're a boss babe extraordinaire who is more than capable."

She nodded sagely and crossed her arms.

And then, due to my painfully obvious nervousness, I continued rambling, "Plus, you seem to know all the good restaurants in town. If you have my number, you can just invite me. I'm getting a little tired of being your sloppy seconds . . . literally. You only eat a second dinner with me after your date crashes and burns, and you usually spill something all over yourself."

"Hey," she accused through her laughter. "I'm part hobbit, okay? And I wear a lot of white. My shirts practically beg to taste my food."

I threw my head back and laughed. God, she was ridiculous. But as I straightened, my gaze traveled down her body. She was, indeed, wearing a bright white tee shirt beneath an oversized striped cardigan that matched her headband. The tee was tucked into high-waist jeans that accentuated her narrow waist. She always looked put together and gorgeous.

I cursed myself for consistently noticing her hair and her red lips and body. But I wasn't quick enough. Gray eyes and a knowing smirk awaited me when I managed to return my gaze to her face.

"Were you staring at my boobs?"

Shiiiiiiit. I could feel my ears going hot. "What? No," I denied. I hadn't *just* been looking at her boobs.

"Yes, you were," she accused again, but she was smiling.

"God. You can't talk about your shirt and expect me not to look."

"I know." She laughed. "I'm just giving you shit." At my glare, she added, "That's what friends do."

I breathed an internal sigh of relief. Perhaps Lu instinctively knew to use the f-word to put us back on safe ground. And thank Christ, we'd stopped talking about her boobs.

"And friends give you artwork for your apartment," I agreed.

"That you are required by law to display," Lu amended.

"That doesn't sound ominous or anything." Not for the first time, I wondered what she'd been compelled to create—something specific just for me. I itched to reach for the paper bag beneath my arm and the art print within.

Lu grinned. "You. Are. Welcome."

We loaded up all the DeLuLu wares in the back of the Bronco and made the short drive to Shady Peaks. Nothing about the day had been as panic-inducing as the surprise run-in with Lu at the General Store. This felt like every other time we'd hung out, grabbing dinner or ice cream after one of Lu's failed first dates. That same easiness, complete with teasing and laughter.

Maybe it was because I'd made a conscious decision to go to the farmers' market. She'd been the sole reason behind the outing, yet no expectations were attached. Everything was casual. I guessed a part of me liked that. Nothing about the day was a blatant shock to the system. Not if I ignored the rapid pace of my heart when Lu smiled at me. Yep, definitely not acknowledging that.

Once all the merch was safely tucked away in Lu's second bedroom, she thanked me for riding to her rescue. I could have said goodbye but lingered in her bright and cozy living room.

Before giving it too much thought, I blurted, "Do you have plans tonight?"

Lu paused in her kitchen, where she was grabbing a clean glass out of the dishwasher. "Uh, no. No plans. Just a quiet night in."

"Would you want to try the pizza-and-movie thing again?"

She watched me for a long moment, perhaps waiting to see if I'd change my mind and bolt from her presence for a third time, but this was okay. It felt safe to be all the way over here. We'd hung out plenty of times, so this wouldn't be any different. I didn't need to make it weird in my brain.

Finally, she said, "Yeah, that sounds good to me. I'm picking the movie, though."

"Fair."

"What do you like on your pizza?"

We didn't end up watching a movie after all. Lu picked a comedy television series from a decade ago that we'd both already seen but found hilarious nonetheless. We shared a ham-and-pineapple pizza and ate on the blue velvet couch.

It was all so easy. She felt like someone I'd known forever. The prospect was both comforting and terrifying.

After we finished the pizza, Lu passed me another beer, and we settled in to keep watching. We laughed amid countless throw pillows while the television played. But after a while, I noticed dwindling laughter and then, finally, quiet coming from the other end of the couch.

I turned to find Lu's head resting on the arm of the sofa and her feet tucked up beneath her. She was breathing deeply, her face soft and relaxed in sleep. The cardigan pulled snuggly around her shoulders.

Rising quietly, I snagged our bottles and emptied them in the kitchen sink. Then I walked back to the couch and grabbed the crocheted blanket draped along the back. I spread it gently over Lu's sleeping form and watched her for a minute.

I felt like I was getting really close to a line. I really hoped I wouldn't go tumbling over it. The last time I'd gotten messed up over a girl, I'd lost everything. While I really liked Lu, I needed to remember to keep some distance there—for my own sake.

Reaching down, I gently brushed back a loose curl that had

fallen across her cheek. Tucking the strand behind her ear, I whispered, "Lu." I didn't want to just leave without saying anything. She didn't stir. "Hey, Tallulah. It's time for me to go." Still nothing. "Wake up, Luanne."

I heard an adorable growl before her gray eyes blinked open. "Not cool, Noah."

Fighting to hide my grin, I told her, "It's late. I need to get home but didn't want to run out on you."

She didn't sit up. Instead, she turned her body to lie flat on her back and stretched out, occupying the space I'd vacated. "I'm glad you stayed."

"Me too. It was fun," I replied, and I meant it. I'd missed Lu while she was in New Mexico. I didn't like it, but there it was.

Maybe I didn't want to let myself rely on anyone in this town because my place here felt tenuous at best.

I was the poster boy for temporary. This girl had hometown sweetheart written all over her.

But something about her kept sneaking past my defenses.

"Good night, Lu. I'll see you."

She smiled, slow and sweet, the edge of sleep trying to pull her back under. "Good night, Noah."

"Lock up after me, okay? Or I'll worry."

"I will, I promise."

I made it to the door when she called out softly, "Noah."

"Yes, Loosey Goosey?"

A sleepy grin lit up her features, and I felt a tug behind my ribs at being the one to put it there. "You know, if you moved here because you're in the mob and need a place to hide out, I promise I won't tell anyone."

I snorted. "Thanks for keeping my mob boss secret." I closed the door to the sound of her soft laughter.

A moment later, I heard the lock click into place and made my way to the parking lot.

The night air was cold in the mountains. I started the Bronco and cranked up the heat, staring out into nothing.

No, I hadn't moved to Cozy Creek because I was running from the mob or in witness protection. It wasn't because I'd inherited a haunted mansion or to study slugs or bees or any of the other ridiculous things Lu had guessed. It was nothing like that.

I'd moved here because my instincts were faulty. When I was desperate and hurting, I'd allowed myself to be taken advantage of. I'd moved to Cozy Creek for a girl—one who hadn't existed, not in any way that mattered. I got catfished by someone I thought cared about me. Instead, she'd kicked me when I was down for nothing more than her own amusement.

Six months ago, I'd met a girl online. I couldn't remember how it started or why I'd matched with someone who lived so far away from my life in South Carolina. But we'd hit it off. Virginia had been fun and interesting, and we'd bonded over living small-town lives and not always loving them.

Eventually, we got to the point where we talked every day—calling or texting, at the very least. Despite never having met in person, I considered her my girlfriend in all the ways that mattered. I wasn't interested in dating anyone else local because I was falling for this girl I'd met online.

One night in early August—just six short weeks ago—one of my help desk employees wasn't able to cover their on-call night shift at work. I'd said I would do it. It wasn't a big deal. Smith Foods was a big corporation, and someone always had to be on call in the office to monitor sensors and warnings and assist store managers in case emergencies cropped up.

I'd arrived at the office to find an issue already in progress, blinking at the top of the alert screen. But Kayleigh, the help desk employee I was relieving, said she'd handled it. Everything was good to go and she'd passed along my direct office number for the store manager to follow up if there were any further issues. There hadn't been. And the main bullpen where tickets came into a bank of monitors was quiet, aside from the flashing alert Kayleigh had handled.

So I'd retreated to my office. Virginia texted and asked for a video call, and I'd figured why not. We'd talked for hours. Virginia told me about her day and an event she was helping her mother put together. She loved sharing her day-to-day with me, and even though we hadn't discussed meeting in person, things felt like they were moving in the right direction.

The night passed quickly, and it wasn't until almost three in the morning that Virginia noticed the time and said she needed to go to bed. We'd said good night, and I'd logged off.

When I'd stepped back out into the bullpen, I noticed the prior alert still flashing. When I looked closer, the issue that Kayleigh took care of before leaving had actually dropped down as complete—hours ago, right after I'd come on shift. The currently blinking ticket had come in immediately after, and I'd missed it, thinking it was the one handled by my employee.

The red flashing alert at the top of the queue was for a refrigerator sensor that detected a significant temperature drop nearly seven hours ago. If I'd noticed the issue right away, I could have notified a field tech in the area. But one hundred and twenty miles away from that rural supermarket, I'd been on a call with my girlfriend and had missed the fucking alert. I'd scrambled at that point, in panic mode. Contacting the store manager had been too late.

The following day, I'd been called into the help desk director's office and fired for my negligence. It hadn't just been a deli cooler or a single freezer that had lost power. The Smith Foods grocery store in Landrum, South Carolina, had their entire stock room refrigeration unit go down due to a bad compressor. I'd missed the alert and hadn't dispatched an on-call technician, and they'd lost tens of thousands of dollars in food.

They'd been right to fire me. I'd cost my company a shit ton of money and liability just so I could talk to my girlfriend.

Completely shell-shocked and wrecked, I'd told Virginia what had happened. Without employment in my hometown, I'd floated the idea of moving closer to her to look for work. A long-distance relationship couldn't last forever, and I'd wanted to be near her.

She'd seemed excited about the future, but when I finally arrived, the truth of our very one-sided relationship came to light.

Virginia had been playing games. Lying and reeling me in for her own twisted entertainment.

When everything had fallen apart, I'd come to Cozy Creek seeking solace and a new beginning. What I'd gotten was a dead end.

I was an idiot, and I had nothing left because I'd been too stupid to see what was right in front of me. I couldn't afford to make the same mistake again.

Reminding myself to be careful where Lu was concerned, I put the Bronco in gear and drove back to my apartment above the bakery.

Hurrying up the back staircase, I unlocked my door and went inside. The paper bag beneath my arm crinkled as I held the DeLuLu Designs bag out in front of me.

I gripped the thick matte and pulled it from the bag, but it wasn't a print like I suspected—like what Lu typically produced. This was watercolor paper and brushstrokes and delicate hand-painted lines. A one-of-a-kind original artwork that was all mine. Why had she done that? Why had Lu made something special just for me?

And then I let my focus zoom out to take in the whole of the painting. My laughter came out in a sharp bark.

Despite the harsh reminder I'd just issued myself, I wondered how I was supposed to resist this girl when she was so . . . everything.

Carrying my new artwork into the bedroom, I propped it up on top of the dresser for the time being. I'd grab a frame for it and hang it soon.

I fought another chuckle as I stared at the cheerful colors and fancy script that read: Live, Laugh, Love.

CHAPTER 6

Lu

The late September day was autumn perfection. The sun was bright and warm, but the breeze carried with it the bite of cooler weather to come. I tugged my oversized scarf a little closer and reveled in the day.

Noah had just dropped me off downtown for my ride request, and I had some time to kill until he picked me up.

I probably could have just texted him to hang out, but despite offering up his number, he still seemed a little skittish. I thought this was the safer route.

It had been almost a week since Noah and I had eaten pizza and watched television in comfortable friendship on my couch. The friendship part was emphasized. It had to be or I'd stare too long at his mouth or do something to scare him off—like ask for another hug.

We'd been in touch throughout the week, texting and swapping funny memes and videos. Surprisingly, we both had a thing for those TikToks of people cleaning obscenely dirty rugs. Who knew?

My phone buzzed in the pocket of my peacoat, and I stepped to the side so that tourists and downtown foot traffic could flow by unobstructed.

Cody: We still on for tonight?

Me: Yes. Drinks at 7

Cody: You bringing your boy?

Me: IDK. Haven't asked yet.

Cody: Worried he won't pass the best friend test?

Me: No, Noah's great. You're going to love him.

Cody: Or are you worried he'll fall in love with me instead?

I snorted.

Me: That is a risk one must accept when having you for a best friend.

Cody: *flips hair* Damn right.

Cody: What Lu did he call you today?

Smiling, I typed, *Luella De Vil.*

Cody: Damn. That's cute.

Me: I KNOOOOWWW

Cody: See you tonight, LuLu.

Cody: BRING HIM!

Smiling, I tucked my phone away. Noah had work and couldn't drink with us at Bookers tonight, but maybe he could stop by and say hi, meet Cody, and pass the best friend test of doom. But I needed to prep Cody and make sure he didn't say anything to make Noah uncomfortable like indicating that I was in love with him. That sort of thing.

I wasn't *in love* with Noah. I just . . . liked him a lot and found him very attractive. But friendship was the name of the game right now, and I was happy to follow Noah's lead.

The prospect of my online dating life left little to be desired on the best of days, but now I'd much rather hang out with Noah. And it was getting easier to ignore my DMs and date requests.

I walked by the visitor center. The marquee advertised our Cozy Creek fall festivities: *Aw shucks! Don't miss out on the corn maze at Sutton Farm. The view is a-maize-ing!*

I grinned. Sonia, who worked in the main office and answered the phones, was adorable and loved a pun.

Maybe Noah might want to check out the farm. I could show him the pumpkin patch. We could take a hayride and grab some apple cider doughnuts. Oh, or the haunted corn maze. I paused, considering. That might be overdoing it.

I'd loved visiting the farm as a kid with my parents. Mom especially loved the various activities, especially the Fall Festival in October. Part of me wanted to relive those memories with my dad, even willing to have a family outing to the farm with Kimberly and Ginny in tow. So far, it hadn't worked out.

That reminded me. I needed to call Kimberly to get the details for Dad's upcoming birthday dinner at Laurel Park Inn. I texted days ago, but my stepmother hadn't responded. Frowning, I pushed aside the hurt that threatened when I thought about how I hadn't been included in my stepmother's plans.

Walking beside the cheerful flower beds filled with bright marigolds and mums, I visited a few of the shops on Main Street. Then I headed toward the Cozy Creek town square, where Noah would be picking me up.

"What's up, Lou Bega? Did you take care of your errands?" My Huber driver awaited, window rolled down and black sunglasses on.

"Yep!" Crossing in front of the Bronco, I noticed the ever-present Igloo cooler was nowhere to be found. So I opened the front passenger door and stuck my head in. "Can I sit up here?"

Noah patted the seat. "Go for it."

I climbed in and took in all the buttons on his dashboard. "Everything looks so different from up here."

He chuckled and shifted into drive. "No, it doesn't, you dork."

I squawked out a surprised laugh and turned my gaze on him. He was in full profile now, so I could see the long line of his lean torso and the way his legs spread beneath the steering wheel. He was relaxed in the driver's seat in his blue jeans and long-sleeved tee shirt.

"What?" he said, still grinning.

"Nothing," I replied, a little flustered at the horny path my thoughts had taken. I faced forward again.

"Am I taking you home?" Noah asked after a moment. We were getting close to the turn for my apartment building.

"Do you have any scheduled rides?"

"Nope. Free as a bird."

I smiled. "You up for a milkshake? I'm buying."

Glancing my way, Noah said, "Why not? Let's do it."

I directed us the short distance to the Shake It Shack on the tail end of Main Street. There was no indoor seating. It was more of a walk-up window, but they had these amazing milkshakes and daily specials that were never repeated. You might find your favorite flavor on the special's placard outside and only get to have it once. Lucky for me, I knew the owner and most of the workers and could get pretty much whatever flavor I wanted.

"Let me order for you," I begged. "I bet I can pick your favorite flavor."

Noah slid his sunglasses up into his brown hair and eyed me skeptically.

"I'm really good at this. Pleeeease," I said, drawing the word out and batting my eyelashes.

"Okay," he relented. "But if I hate it, I get to drink yours."

"Deal."

After grabbing a hazelnut mocha milkshake for myself and a coconut cream pie one for Noah, we hopped back in the Bronco.

I turned in the front seat to stare at Noah as he pulled out into

Main Street traffic.

Glancing my way, he did a double take. "Why are you staring at me?"

"Take a sip."

He raised a skeptical brow. "You're being weird. Is it poisoned?"

Huffing in exasperation, I quickly replied, "No, I just want to see if you like it. Go on. Try it."

Noah waited until we stopped at the traffic light before slowly lifting his milkshake from the cup holder and bringing the straw to his lips. I watched as his mouth parted around the plastic and his cheeks hollowed, sucking in the thick mixture until he could taste it on his tongue. He made no outward sign as he swallowed.

"What do you think?" I asked, practically bouncing in my seat.

"It's good," he finally replied around another long swallow.

I eyed him skeptically as he pulled into the parking lot of Shady Peaks. He grabbed a space for the Bronco close to my building and shifted into park.

We sat, drinking our milkshakes in his car, the only sounds were our straws squeaking in tandem. I let it go for another thirty seconds before I held my cup out to him.

Snatching it out of the air, he sighed, "Thank God."

My shoulders were shaking with repressed laughter as I accepted his coconut cream pie milkshake. "Were you just going to suffer through the whole thing?"

"I'm sorry! I don't like coconut. Something about the texture is like hair in my mouth. But this," he acknowledged around a sip, "is amazing."

I watched him with a smirk but didn't say anything.

Hazel eyes slid my way. "You did that on purpose, didn't you?"

"I said I could pick your favorite. I didn't say I'd order it for you."

"Diabolical," he accused, then drew on the straw again. "Delicious."

"I use my powers mostly for good," I claimed. "I just wanted to see what you'd do. If you'd immediately admit you hated the coconut shake or if you'd hide it from me to spare my delicate feelings."

He hummed around his straw. My gaze strayed to where his lips wrapped around the plastic—where my own lips had been just moments ago. His cheekbones were more pronounced as he worked to get to the sweetness inside. With my eager eyes, I traced the flexing of his jaw and the column of his throat as he swallowed.

"What?" he finally asked, breaking me out of my inappropriate ogling.

Damn. I needed to get it together. "Nothing," I squeaked, forcing my attention out the front window. "Actually, I was going to invite you tonight," I decided and said simultaneously. "Cody and I are grabbing drinks at Bookers, the pub and grill on Main Street, if you get a break and want to drop by. I know you can't have alcohol while you're working, but you could finally meet Cody and hang out until you needed to pick someone up."

Noah nodded. "Yeah, that sounds good."

I smiled, happy that he'd agreed so readily. Cody would be

thrilled. "I'll probably head over around seven."

"Do you need a ride?" He took another distracting gulp of his milkshake.

"No," I said, feeling a prickle of guilt. "Cody's picking me up." Why was I being weird about this? I could just tell him. I didn't have to be dishonest.

I must have stared too long in shameful contemplation because Noah laughed and said, "You're staring again."

Quickly glancing away, I attempted to bring balance to the force. "Just thinking about why you moved here."

"Oh yeah?" I could tell he was smiling. He knew this game we played.

Feeling the flush on my cheeks, I took a quick sip of my shake—Noah's shake—to steady my sudden horny nerves. "Yeah, you heard about local legend and movie star Grayson Ames. You moved here to try to stake out the town for when he comes home for the Fall Festival and to grand marshal the Christmas parade."

I could feel Noah's attention on the side of my face. "Grayson Ames is really from here?"

"Yep. Went to Cozy Creek High School and everything. He was a few years ahead of me, though. He's a really nice guy and has done a lot for the town. His family is pretty great, too."

"Wow," Noah replied. I still couldn't will myself to make eye contact with him. "I love his movies. Small world."

"Small world," I agreed.

"Not so much the draw of Grayson Ames—great though it may be—but I've been working on setting up a web design business."

Desperately trying to be chill about this freely given information, I turned my head to look at Noah. It wasn't the reason he'd moved here. He wasn't quite giving me that, but it was something—something personal. Those details had been pretty sparse so far.

"That sounds cool," I replied, my mind already spinning and thinking how amazing this could be. "Really cool actually. There are so many businesses that would benefit from having their own websites. Amari could use more than a social media page with infrequent updates. The visitor center and the town, for that matter, need a centralized website to promote activities and events. It could really impact tourism."

I could feel myself talking faster the more enthusiastic I got. Noah could have clients in town. He could have a successful business and help others. It would make him a part of Cozy Creek—a real part.

Noah looked thoughtful as he sipped his milkshake and listened to me babble excitedly. "That . . . gives me a lot to think about. Thank you."

I beamed at him.

"I'm still in the planning stages," he said in that same slow, cautious tone.

"That's fine. I love planning stages. Let me know when you're ready to move forward. I can help."

His smile was genuine and sweet, that almost-worried look slowly melting from his features as his eyes moved over my face, caressing every part. "You are a really nice person."

I felt warm under his sudden praise. Compliments didn't come around like that every day. It was normal to have someone comment on your hair or your clothes, but those were just outward things. When someone praised your character and your heart, well, that was special and rare. "I like to think so. Well, I hope I am."

"You are," Noah insisted, his voice low and soft. Those hazel eyes lingered, touching my cheekbones with reverence, carefully following the line of my jaw before landing heavily on my lips. "I'd forgotten that good people still existed."

Confusion washed over me, along with a heavy frown. What did he mean by that? Who had hurt Noah so badly that he'd lost faith in people?

Before I could wonder those thoughts aloud, Noah shifted closer, leaning over the center console and cupping my cheek.

My eyes widened in surprise, but I leaned into his touch, meeting him halfway.

His fingers slid into my hair and flexed a little as if they couldn't help themselves, gently clutching the strands. Then Noah's thumb brushed against my cheekbone over and over, making my heart race.

I ached to cradle his jaw or run my fingers through his brown hair in return, but somehow I knew that whatever magic had instigated this closeness was tenuous and fragile. One wrong move might break the spell and have Noah's walls slamming into place, leaving me painfully alone on the other side.

Hazel eyes caressed every inch of my face before landing on

my lips. Finally, Noah's eyes drifted shut and his mouth met mine in a spark of tender heat. Our lips parted and slotted together, my bottom lip caught between his.

He tasted dark and delicious, like chocolate. The scruff of his short beard was rough and welcome, lighting up my senses and making me eager to feel it everywhere—along my throat and collarbone and lower still.

Our mouths moved together in a slow dance. He led, and I followed, feeling dizzy from his touch. This was what I'd been wanting. What I'd been waiting for. All our comfortable conversation and simmering attraction were leading us here, together. I'd known we had something more between us. It was rare to feel an instant connection with another person. From that very first Huber ride, meeting Noah had felt like a gift. We just clicked.

Yes, we would be great friends, but more was waiting just beneath the surface. And this was the beginning.

A loud buzz to my right had us jolting apart. I giggled a little as Noah groaned, palming his face roughly before grabbing his phone out of the dashboard holder. A text from Jimmy Huber was lit up on the screen. Looked like Noah had a new ride request.

"I should, uh, get going," Noah said, gaze fixed on his phone, refusing to meet mine.

Unease started as a tiny whisper before it became a dull roar.

"Okay," I replied slowly in confusion, watching him stare unseeingly at the dark screen before him. "I'll talk to you later?"

Noah sighed, finally lifting his eyes to look at me. He looked resigned and . . . sorry. "Listen, Lu."

"Oh." I interrupted, my mood abruptly nosediving into the sea. "I think that is the fastest letdown in the history of letdowns." I was already reaching to the floorboard for my bag, trying not to be the emotional girl who'd let her heart get away from her head.

"Lu," he tried again. "I'm sorry. I shouldn't have kissed you. It was a mistake. I'm not in a position to—"

His apology and excuses were white noise in the background of my frantic attempt to exit this vehicle with my embarrassment and pride imploding like a star and sucking me in.

"Got it," I mumbled, focusing on opening and closing the passenger door with appropriate force—not hysterical-girl force that wanted me to slam his stupid fucking door for making me feel like such an idiot.

He had kissed *me*. I didn't need to feel bad. It wasn't some signal I'd missed. He'd been the one to lean in. Noah had looked at me all dreamy and then slid smoothly across the threshold of friendship. Yet I was the one fighting tears of frustration and hurt while he called *me* a mistake.

Noah didn't reach out for me again.

I couldn't believe how wrong I'd been. Here I was, pushing— always pushing. Trying to make this guy like me. Wanting him to love this town. I would have done anything to banish that wounded, sad-boy look from his face. But whatever I'd been doing hadn't been enough. Or maybe it was too much. I didn't know.

What I did know was that I'd been wrong. Noah and I weren't going anywhere, after all. Whatever path I thought we'd been on had been wishful thinking because Noah had thrown up a road-block that I couldn't even see around.

"Well, aren't you a ray of sunshine?" Cody eyed me as I threw my bag down and dropped into the booth across from him.

"Sorry," I mumbled.

My best friend's dark brows were still raised in surprise as he watched me get settled. "Do you want to talk about it?"

"No," I grumbled. "Not yet anyway."

He slid his margarita in front of me.

I picked up the drink and took three gulps before placing it back on the table.

Cody's eyebrows had gone absolutely nowhere. "What about now?"

"Maybe." My response was petulant and grouchy. It wasn't Cody's fault that I was in a bad mood. He hadn't blown me off. He was here, being the amazing, supportive friend he always was.

Cody and I had met in college as freshmen who were still trying to figure things out. We'd formed a tight-knit trio after meeting Emma in an Intro to Psychology class during our first semester on campus. We'd eventually become roommates, and having two amazing best friends had helped heal my tender heart.

At the time, college had been an escape. I'd desperately need-ed to get out of Cozy Creek. My mother's death and my father's subsequent decision to remarry so soon afterward made my last two years in high school the most difficult of my life.

A fresh start and a town without so many reminders of all the things I'd lost helped me find myself again. And Cody and Emma had given me the companionship I desperately needed.

We'd supported each other through so much. I was unbelievably grateful that Cody had chosen to relocate to Cozy Creek after graduation. He was the pastry chef at the Cozy Creek Lodge. His dream was to own his own bakery. He had the business degree and the baking talent to make it happen. He was just saving money and waiting for the right time to leave his current position. But it was hard. A lot of people depended on him. And part of me worried that with his crush on the executive chef at the Lodge, he'd never find the motivation or the wherewithal to step away. A night off like tonight was very rare.

And I shouldn't be ruining it with my shitty attitude.

I took in Cody's pale elegant button-up that stood out against his warm brown skin and his black hair, parted on the side and styled in a trendy swoop. Either my BFF was on the prowl for a guy or he'd pulled out all the stops to make a good impression on Noah—for me. That thought made my stomach twist. There was no way Noah would show up now.

"Noah kissed me and then said it was a mistake," I admitted before bringing the margarita back up to my mouth.

Somehow, Cody's artfully manicured eyebrows managed to go even higher. "Okay, tell me everything."

So I did. Over another round, I relayed the milkshakes and our conversation. The kiss and the interruption. I confided in Cody. I told him how Noah had said it was all a mistake. That *I* had been a mistake.

"You know he's just afraid, right?" my friend said immediately. "Something in that boy's past has him running scared. It has nothing to do with you, LuLu. You're perfect."

"Pfffft." I might have been a little drunk.

"And," Cody continued as if I hadn't made a rude noise of disagreement, "I bet you anything, it has to do with why he's in town. It wouldn't be a secret if it didn't hurt."

I considered that. Noah had let me keep guessing, each reason more ridiculous than the last. But he'd never told me the truth. It had been weeks now. Why was he still hiding?

Shaking my head, I said, "It doesn't matter. If he doesn't want to open up to me, I can't force him. I wouldn't want to do that anyway." What good was trust if it wasn't earned?

"Soooo, what? You're just giving up on him? Gonna duck behind bushes when you see his Bronco go rolling down the street?"

Despite my melancholy, I laughed at that imagery. I was definitely a little drunk. "What's the alternative? I'm embarrassed, okay. I kissed him back. I like him. I want to kiss him again. I thought we had something—something special. A connection. I don't know. But we're clearly not on the same page."

Cody looked disbelieving. "I just can't see you giving up on this guy altogether. Not with the way you talked about him. What if he wanted to go back to being friends? Oh! What if he can't go around kissing you?" He lowered his voice and hissed,

"What if he has a girlfriend?"

That made me pause.

I shouldn't have kissed you. It was a mistake. I'm not in a position to—"

God. What if Noah *did* have a girlfriend? I'd never even considered that. He'd never mentioned anyone, and we'd been hanging out so much. Surely, a girlfriend wouldn't be okay with that.

"What if they're long distance?" Cody said, reading the direction of my panicked thoughts. "He moved here for . . . something. Whatever. But she's back in South Carolina."

Thumping my head on the back of the booth, I mumbled, "Oh crap."

Cody met my eyes and mouthed, "Home-wrecker."

"Oh my God. Stop!" But I laughed a little and threw a lime wedge at his head.

"Not my hair," he squawked, looking around the bar to see if anyone noticed.

I smiled. "No more mopey Lu. I'm sorry I'm ruining our night."

"Honey, this is what best friends are for. Your dating life has been woefully uninspiring. I'm sorry it didn't work out with Noah Sad Boy, but now you can put him behind you." I made to protest but Cody kept right on talking. "Stay friends or whatever. But go back to online dating and trying to find Mr. Right. I know you slacked off while you were dealing with the whole Noah infatuation. But now he's not a distraction anymore. You can focus on you, LuLu."

Focus on me. Go back to swiping right, dick pics in my DMs,

and no-show first dates.

Great.

I didn't want to be lonely forever. I wanted a family—a partner. I wanted to feel a connection with someone.

Like how I felt with Noah.

Well, I guess I wasn't going to find what I was looking for if I didn't actually put some effort into the search.

I nodded, but Cody didn't notice. He was eyeing some guy at the bar with a really nice beard.

"You're right," I said, drawing his attention.

"Of course, I'm right. Give it a few days to let the sting wear off, and then get back on that horse."

The horse sounded terrible, but Cody made a good point. I might miss out on someone amazing while busy pining over someone who didn't even want me.

I didn't know if Noah would even still want to be friends or if I could manage that. But I thought about how he seemed all alone in this town. It was true. I couldn't make Noah care about me. And he was wrong to have instigated something if he did, indeed, have a girlfriend.

But the idea of losing Noah altogether made me feel terrible. It felt wrong. If Noah needed a friend, I could do my best to be that for him. I could try to put aside my romantic feelings and be what he needed. I couldn't just give up on him.

I sighed and considered ordering a third margarita.

And to no one's surprise, Noah didn't show up for drinks.

CHAPTER 7

Lu

"She was a total bitch about it. So we broke up. That doesn't mean she needs to keep calling me and key my fucking car."

I stared in horror as my date continued his play-by-play of his recent breakup around open-mouthed bites of mozzarella sticks. "We were only together for four years. It's not like we were married."

Leighton's phone buzzed on the table, and he rolled his eyes before snatching it up. "There she is again." But his thumbs tapped out a reply for—I checked my phone—two minutes and twelve seconds.

"I told her I had a date tonight," he groused, reaching for a cheese stick as our server delivered another Jack and Coke. "That's definitely why she's texting. Trying to get under my skin."

I tried to make eye contact with the young twentysomething server to, I don't know, commiserate or signal that he should maybe stop serving this guy, but no such luck.

"Breakups are hard," I offered weakly, feeling dread pool in my stomach.

I hadn't wanted to be here in the first place. It had been over a week since the kiss with Noah. I hadn't heard from him or seen him at all. Cody had encouraged me to hit the dating scene again and let the thing with Noah go. It had sounded reasonable at the time.

The guy I'd agreed to meet tonight, Leighton Brody, had seemed pretty innocuous on paper—well, on the dating app. Sandy hair and big brown eyes gave him a boyish look, but his beard was giving eighties stockbroker vibes along with the white blazer he wore. He was employed at a bank and worked in Balfour, the next town over. In our brief texting exchange a few days ago, he hadn't seemed like a complete douchebag who'd just gotten out of a long-term relationship. But here we were.

Leighton ignored me and kept up the steady stream of complaints about his ex. "I *told* her I wasn't ready to get married and have kids. I mean, come on. I'm only thirty-four."

Well, his profile said he was twenty-eight, so I felt like I was misled in the relationship as well.

The server returned with an impatient stare and asked what we'd like to order.

"No rush, my man," my date replied cheerfully and then held up his glass. "Grab me another on your way back while we browse the menu."

The server took off with a sigh, and my eyes nearly bulged out of my head as Leighton drained his second drink.

There was no way I would make it through dinner with this asshole. On the other hand, he'd need the food to absorb some of the alcohol so we could eventually leave this restaurant. Inwardly, I cursed myself for agreeing to let Leighton pick me up. I sure as shit wasn't going to call for a Huber and have to see Noah again when he clearly didn't want to talk to me. The text he'd left on read three days ago proved that.

Maybe I could just drive Leighton's car and take him home to sleep it off. And then grab a ride from my dad or Cody back to town. My friend should be off work by then, even if my dad was busy. I'd have to figure it out because I didn't want Leighton driving drunk.

His phone continued buzzing and lighting up on the table. Between polishing off his third drink and the remaining mozzarella sticks, my date engaged in a heated exchange with his former girlfriend that required all of his attention and focus.

Thank God.

This was by far the worst first date I'd ever been on. I'd take the no-shows and the ghosting midmeal to this horrible experience any day. Hell, even that guy and his mom had been better company than this. No one wanted to listen to someone complain about their ex for—I checked my phone again—forty-eight minutes and counting. And I hadn't even gotten one of those mozzarella sticks.

"You know what, Leighton?" His gaze stayed fixed on his phone.

I tried again. "Leighton."

The jerk had the nerve to hold up a finger and mumble, "Give me a minute here."

Huffing an angry breath, I imagined myself shooting a fireball out of my nostrils. Nothing was worth this. I'd be single forever. Get some plants and an army of cats before I ever settled for this guy.

Leighton reached blindly for another mozzarella stick but he'd already eaten them all and looked up in confusion when his hand came up empty.

"So," I said, drawing his attention away from the appetizer plate in the middle of the table. "I think we should call it a night."

His dark eyes narrowed in my direction. "Yeah, that's probably for the best. I'm not feeling this. You're not really my type."

I put my hands in my lap to avoid lunging for the butter knife sitting on the tabletop.

"Right," I gritted out. "So if you want to just hand me your keys, I'll drive you home and catch a ride back to Cozy Creek."

Leighton scoffed. "You can't drive my baby."

I wanted to roll my eyes. He'd picked me up in a two-seater red sports car that was completely impractical for living in the mountains. It had been so low to the ground that if I hadn't been wearing tights under my dress, I would have flashed innocent bystanders while I climbed out of the car.

"Listen," I replied calmly despite how tempting that butter

knife still looked. "You just pounded three drinks in less than an hour. If you try to drive out of here, I'll call the sheriff's office. You can let me drive, or you can call for a ride for yourself. But I'm not getting in a vehicle with you behind the wheel, and I'm not letting you endanger other motorists."

"Other motorists," he mimicked in a high voice. "Listen to you. You're still not driving my car. You probably can't even drive a stick. We can call for a ride."

God, he was infuriating.

I paid the bill just to move things along.

It wasn't until we stood on the sidewalk in front of the restaurant that drunk Leighton seemed to realize he couldn't just request a ride-share from his phone app. "There are no drivers nearby. How is that possible?"

Because Cozy Creek is too small and out of the way to warrant popular ride-share chains. But I didn't say any of that. I had my phone up to my ear, praying my dad hadn't already turned in for the night. My hopes didn't immediately sink, though. Not until Cody didn't answer either, instead, he texted me to say he was still at work at the Lodge and would call me in two hours when he finished the prep work for the following day.

Cody: I can't wait to hear all about your date!

A growl might have left my throat.

I swallowed uncomfortably when I realized we didn't have a lot of options. "Can you get a hold of anyone to come get you?" I asked, my voice losing hope the longer we stood out in the frigid night air. "Maybe your ex?" Since she was apparently available to keep up a constant barrage of text messages.

"I am not calling that bitch for anything."

Okay then. Once a douchebag, always a douchebag.

I could walk home. It was a couple of miles, but I could do it. However, I didn't really trust this guy to get home without wrapping his midlife crisis mobile around a tree or hurting some innocent person in the process. It was a twenty-five-minute drive to Balfour, at least. A lot could happen on the dark roads between here and there.

"Give me your address," I said sharply enough to get Leighton's attention. He obliged and then went back to ignoring me.

With a resigned sigh, I navigated to my recent call list and found the number I was looking for. After relaying the pertinent information, I sat on the curb and tucked my skirt around my legs. It was nearly October, and the nights were crisp and cold. About a million stars twinkled in the sky, but I couldn't enjoy the sight. I wished I had a hot chocolate. I wished I was at a bonfire with a blanket wrapped around my shoulders. I wished I was home on my couch. Basically anywhere but here with Leighton the Douchebagface ™ while I awaited my depressing fate.

"Our ride will be here in a few minutes," I said after Leighton dropped to sit next to me. His attention was already back on his phone.

This was quite literally the last place I wanted to be.

Noah

I stared at the ride request from Jimmy and then stared some more.

The pickup location was the same restaurant I'd taken Lu to weeks ago—our very first ride. But the destination was not Lu's apartment nearby. It was an address over in Balfour. Navigation said it was twenty-eight minutes away.

With my mind spinning and dread gathering, I pulled into the parking lot of the upscale restaurant, and everything became a whole lot clearer. Lu waited outside with another man, and suddenly, all my disappointment solidified into something bitter and resentful.

I'd been beating myself up for over a week. And then when Lu had texted me a few days ago, I'd stared at it like a moron. I'd kept staring at it. Looking at my phone randomly and wishing I was braver or smarter or someone she deserved.

Can we talk?

That was it. Unexpected after the way I'd freaked out on her but there it was—a lifeline cast out in the middle of the ocean. Three words that had me simultaneously spiraling and hopeful. She hadn't written me off.

Every time I picked up my phone and stared at Lu's text, I thought about replying, telling her I was sorry. That I never should have said I regretted kissing her. She hadn't deserved that. Kissing her had been amazing, life-changing, perfection. And she was perfect, too. I was the one who was so fucked up.

I was too scared to trust myself and too scared to trust her either.

But as I stopped in front of the sidewalk in front of the restaurant, I thought I might have made the right decision after all. Whatever this was, it made me feel foolish to have been mooning over her text message. It made me feel spiteful and angry, too. It was clear that Lu hadn't been staring at *her* phone, hoping for a response. She'd been making other plans instead, and I had no one to blame but myself.

Lu rose gracefully to her feet, but the guy beside her wobbled enough that my eyes darted to hers in surprise. She was ignoring him, though, already on her way to my window as her companion stumbled toward the Bronco.

I hit the button to lower the barrier between us, and she rushed out, "Noah, I'm sorry to make you come here. But this whole thing is not what you—"

Whatever she wanted to say was lost in the sounds of pretentious asshole as her date struggled into the back seat. "Man, not much room back here."

I nearly rolled my eyes. The guy was maybe five feet eight inches. He'd survive the lack of legroom.

"Noah—" Lu was interrupted again by the guy who I assumed was her date.

"Let's get this show on the road, sweetheart!"

Even in the dimness of the parking lot, I could see her face flush scarlet. So I turned my gaze forward and set up navigation to take us to the address I'd been given.

Lu stood beside my window for another eleven seconds before giving up and getting in the back seat.

I resisted the urge to glance at her in my rearview mirror.

What was she doing here with this idiot? And why was she calling me—the guy she'd kissed a week ago—to come and get her? Was she trying to make me jealous?

I didn't like games, and everything about this scenario gave me a bad feeling.

Pulling back out onto the road, I turned the Bronco in the direction of Balfour. The interior of the vehicle was painfully quiet. The vibe was all off, and I had no idea what was happening. Nothing about Lu and this mystery guy felt like they'd been on a date or even knew each other. But I had to assume I was driving them somewhere together—possibly his house.

Why was Lu going home with this guy? They weren't even talking. His face was illuminated by the phone in his grip holding all his attention. Lu was staring out the window at the view rushing by on the two-lane highway. Maybe he was someone in her family—her stepfamily that treated her like garbage?

But that theory went out the window when I heard Lu pipe up from the back seat a moment later. "What—what are you doing?"

"Shhh," the guy whispered and then giggled like the drunk dumbass he was. "Come here."

"Um, no." Shoes shuffled on the floorboard. "What are you— no, stop it." My eyes flew to the mirror, but it was dark. There were sounds of clothes rustling and more scrambling.

I sat up straighter. "Hey."

But Lu was already screeching, "Leighton, Jesus, get your hands off me."

Well, that was clear enough. The bright lights of a gas station were fast approaching on my right. I made sure there was no one behind me and slammed on my brakes to slow us enough to swing into the lot of the convenience store.

Throwing the Bronco in park, I jumped out and went around to the asshole's door. Wrenching it open, I grabbed the back of a ridiculous white blazer and pulled the guy out of the back seat and away from Lu.

"What the fuck do you think you're doing?" He stumbled back, arms windmilling before he landed hard on his ass.

"She told you to stop, dipshit. Now you can walk home." I peered over my shoulder and saw Lu standing near the back of the SUV, arms crossed and features as closed off and angry as I'd ever seen them. "Unless you want to press charges, Lu? We can call it in."

"No, I want to go home."

"You have got to be kidding me," he snarled from the ground.

"You're lucky I'm leaving you here instead of the side of the highway."

"Fuck you," he spat, still making no attempt to get off the ground.

I heard Lu's door close and gave the asshole one more look that said *I will back over you with my car and not feel bad about it* before I went back to the driver's side and climbed in.

After I shifted into drive and turned back toward Cozy Creek,

I cleared the residual anger from my throat and asked into the quiet between us, "Are you okay?"

"Yeah. I'm fine. He was just drunk and handsy all of a sudden." I watched Lu tug the ends of her coat tighter around herself before focusing back on the road. "This wasn't how things were supposed to go tonight. I just want you to know that I didn't mean—"

"It's okay," I said, interrupting whatever explanation she felt like she owed me. The truth was, Lu didn't owe me anything. She'd had a shitty night with another loser first date. But she *had* gone on another date.

Yes, I was the idiot who'd kissed her and then said it was a mistake. I'd initiated something I had no business following through on.

I didn't expect Lu to sit around and pine for me. That would have been selfish and hypocritical. But seeing her waiting on the curb tonight with that guy had done something to me. Knowing that she'd called for a ride, knowing it would be me who showed up . . . well, it hurt. Thinking I was taking her back to his place made me remember that I didn't like being toyed with.

When women got bored and decided to play games with me, I ended up the loser, every time.

"It's okay?" Lu repeated my words, voice incredulous. "That's all?"

My hands tightened around the steering wheel reflexively. "I don't know what you want me to say, Lu. I'm glad you're okay. I'm taking you home. That's my job."

"Your job," she replied quietly. I could see her nodding to herself when I glanced in the rearview mirror.

I forced myself to loosen my grip on the wheel and reposition my hands.

Silence stretched between us, and I had no one to blame but myself. I didn't feel any better when I pulled into Shady Peaks.

For once, Lu had cash ready and waiting. She didn't need to dig around in her massive purse. She laid the folded bills for the cost of her ride on my center console. "Thanks for tonight."

And before I could reply, she was out of the Bronco and striding toward her building.

Hitting the button, I lowered my window on instinct. A word rose in my throat but never made it past my lips.

Lu kept her head down and marched into her building as regret crept in along with the night air.

I didn't tell her to stop. I let her walk away instead.

My phone buzzed with an incoming text from Jimmy, but I didn't drive away until I saw the light click on in the apartment I knew was Lu's. I knew because I'd been in there. We'd spent time together. Become friends. And then I'd fucked it all up by kissing her, thinking about possibilities and a future in this tiny town.

Maybe we could have made it as friends for a while. Ignored the attraction we both felt. I could have pretended I didn't notice that string that connected us—the one that made every encounter feel like a sunlamp was warming me from the inside out. Maybe I could have disregarded all the complicated feelings I had for Luanne Billings. For a while at least.

But I wouldn't get a chance to test the theory. I'd pushed her away and run her off. Friendship wasn't even in the cards for us anymore.

It was better this way. We could stop before anyone got really hurt. And before the pretending became impossible.

I knew it was for the best, but as I sat there watching that rectangle of warm golden light, I felt the loss of her like a wound— my reality going cold and numb.

CHAPTER 8

Noah

I looked from the sidewalk to the name on my ride request and could not believe this was happening all over again.

With her hair up in a messy bun, Lu stood outside of Bookers next to a dark-haired, well-dressed man.

This was the bar she'd invited me to a few weeks ago before we'd kissed and everything had gone to shit.

Despite all the similarities between the last time I'd seen Lu and now, there were differences, too. She was surprised to see me. So requesting a Huber hadn't been her idea. The guy at her side wasn't short or drunk, but he was still ignoring her.

As soon as she'd spotted the Bronco idling out front, she'd tried to turn around and march back inside, but the guy—I checked my phone again—Dakota had snagged her around the waist. If body language was anything to go by, she was going to kill him.

I was both desperate to get this over with and also grateful for the chance to see her. It had been exactly one week since I'd picked up Lu and her handsy first date, not knowing what to think about everything but feeling heartsick over it.

Lowering my window, I called, "Are you Dakota Marshall?"

The man—probably around Lu's age—smiled brightly. His teeth were insanely white. "That's me!" And then with a threat reminiscent of a mother wrangling her wayward toddler, he said, "Come on, LuLu. Get in the car."

She met my gaze, and I realized she wanted to be anywhere else but in front of this bar at three in the morning. She didn't look drunk or disheveled, just reluctant. And just before she glanced away, I caught the edge of something that looked a lot like regret.

Dakota tugged her along by the arm of her peacoat before opening the back passenger door and stuffing her inside, giant handbag and all.

I tried to make myself focus on the navigation system and where I was supposed to be driving instead of noticing every little sound Lu made in the back seat—the uncomfortable shift of her body, the way she held herself against the door, her sigh as she looked out the window.

"First stop is me," Dakota said once he'd climbed in behind me. "Then you can drop LuLu at home."

Some furious whispering ensued as I pulled out onto the deserted Main Street. I caught a "jackass" and "too bad" followed by a "never" and then a "be that way."

As agonizing as it had been to see Lu on a date with that asshole last week, I could tell pretty quickly that she wasn't into him. It was more the possibility. I'd realized that if I didn't get out of this town soon, someday I was going to have to pick up this girl and watch her give her smiles and her attention to someone else.

It had been a relief to recognize easily that the phone-obsessed handsy asshole was not someone who Lu was giving the time of day. But something *was* there with this Dakota guy. Familiarity and comfort. Acceptance and understanding. These two had a history, and I wasn't sure how to feel about that.

"So, Noah," he said, "it's nice to finally meet you. I'm sorry it has to be under these dramatic circumstances."

Lu practically growled.

"Uhhh . . . " That was all I could manage because I had no idea what the hell was going on.

"I'm Cody," he offered.

Cody.

Oh.

That Cody. Lu's best friend Cody.

My eyes flicked to his in the back seat. He was smiling that megawatt grin. "Oh, um, hi."

Why did he still want to meet me? He had to know things with Lu were complicated and practically on life support.

"How has your night been?" Cody asked in a friendly tone. I

guessed we were chatting. What the hell?

My eyes took a quick detour to see Lu glaring out the window, ignoring whatever Cody was doing.

"It's been pretty quiet. Busy earlier, but nothing too bad."

"Good," Cody replied cheerfully. "That's good."

"Yeah." This was so weird. I checked the time left until arrival: eight minutes. Fantastic.

"So, here's the thing," Cody said, shifting into serious gear, "you and Lu need to get your shit together." I felt my eyebrows disappear beneath my hair. "I was on your side, Noah Sad Boy. But I can't have you hurting my girl. Tonight was painful," he groaned, drawing the last word out. "She had tourists all over her. LuLu could have left with twelve numbers in her pocket and a 'why choose' situation to end the night."

I did not know what that meant. And I didn't think I wanted to.

"But no," Cody continued. "She moped all over the damn bar. Worst wingwoman ever. I could have gone home with three different guys." Oh. *Ohhhhhh.* "But I felt bad leaving her pathetic ass. She didn't even drink. She had ginger ale and a bowl full of maraschino cherries because the bartender felt sorry for her."

I swallowed uncomfortably and glanced in the rearview mirror, attempting to read Lu's expression. She stared at her friend in shock, heavy on the betrayal.

Unbothered, Cody went on, "So I will say again. You two crazy kids need to figure your shit out. You are clearly into her—I saw your 'wounded puppy' eyes when you saw us on the sidewalk—and she is into you—hush, LuLu—but for whatever reason, you've decided to make each other miserable instead. You are going to drop me off, and then you are going to talk. Okay?"

A small part of me wanted to stand up to Cody and tell him he didn't know anything about me and to back off. But I wasn't brave enough to do that because Cody was more than a little scary. And also right. I was miserable. And I was into Lu.

I'd spent the past week moping, simultaneously hoping to run into her and praying I wouldn't. My head was a mess, but I missed her—missed the easiness and comfort between us.

"Okay," I agreed after a moment.

"Good," Cody replied, cheerful once more. "I'm on the right."

I pulled to a stop where he'd indicated. The house was a nice two-story Victorian that looked like it had been split into several apartment units.

"You'll forgive me," Cody said before kissing Lu on the cheek. He tossed some cash into the front passenger seat and leaned forward. "Do better, Sad Boy Noah." And then he unfolded from the Bronco and made his way down the front path and through the front door of the Victorian.

Lu and I sat in tense silence until I mustered up the courage and said, "Do you want to go somewhere and talk?"

When I didn't get an answer, I turned in my seat to see Lu staring down at her lap, fingers twisted together anxiously. "I'm sorry about Cody. You don't need to worry about him. And you shouldn't let him force you into doing something—"

"He's not," I interrupted. "I would like to talk. If you do," I quickly amended. "You shouldn't feel coerced."

"That's okay. We can talk."

Hope didn't take flight in my chest, but it did get off the ground.

"There's an overlook not far from here," she went on. "Where people have photos taken. It'll be quiet since it's so late. Unless you need to get back."

"Nah, I'm off duty. This is my last ride of the night. Lead the way."

Lu guided me several miles up the mountain. The scenic overlook was near the gondola station, and it was, indeed, abandoned at 3:18 a.m. But I could see the mountains surrounding us in the dark gray night. Stars glittered in the sky, the moon highlighting snow on the highest peaks. There was something very serene about being surrounded by so much untamed nature. The solidity helped calm my racing heart when I thought about the woman in my back seat.

"This is amazing."

"Yeah," she agreed. "It's one of my favorite spots. My mom loved it here. Sometimes we'd come at night and look at the stars."

She'd mentioned her mom before, so I knew the basics of how she'd lost her far too young. And now, I could hear the wistful sadness in her voice and felt grateful that she'd shared someplace so special with me.

"Do you want to come up here and sit with me?"

She hummed and then said, "I think you should sit in the back.

See what it's like for the rest of us."

Switching off the headlights, I turned the heat up a little and moved to join Lu.

I got settled in the back seat, and after the sounds of the door closing and fabric shifting, the silence felt loaded. However misguided, there was an expectation of being in the back seat with Lu. My mind knew it, and so did my body. I felt tense and aware of every single thing. Our proximity. The sweet vanilla scent that clung to her skin. How warm and close and dialed up my awareness became when she was within inches.

Eventually, I managed to say, "So . . . Cody."

Lu snorted a laugh. Her head dropped back against the headrest, and she released a sigh that I felt against my cheek. "God, he's a monster." But there was so much affection in her voice. It was the kind of exasperation you could only feel for someone you loved in your bones.

Nerves and tension had me wiping my palms down the thighs of my jeans. "You guys never . . . "

She glanced over in horror. "No. We've been best friends for years—since our first year of college. And he's not into me or *any* woman that way."

I nodded, remembering what he'd said about Lu being a shitty wingwoman tonight.

Lu's gaze stayed fixed on my face, and before I had the chance to ask her what was wrong, she blurted out, "Can I just say something about last week? I wasn't going home with him—Leighton. Dinner was awful. *He* was awful," she insisted, her expression pained.

"He got drunk before he even finished his appetizer, so I asked to leave. But then he wouldn't let me drive his precious car. I tried calling my dad for a ride. But he—he couldn't get me." Her words were pouring out of her in a frantic rush. "I didn't know what else to do, okay? I couldn't just walk home and leave him there to get in his car and kill somebody out on the road, so I called for a ride. I asked Jimmy to come himself, but he was at a family dinner at his sister's."

"Oh," I said, following her flood of honesty. I hadn't been expecting any of that and wasn't sure what to think.

Lu continued. "I didn't even want to be out with him. I was hurt over what happened with us and felt desperate. Like I was never going to meet someone who wanted me. I thought if I moved us back into the friend zone, I could stay in your life, but you ignored my text and I didn't deal with it well."

My spinning thoughts touched on a million different things: her date, the realization that her dad had let her down again, but mostly, I focused on the fact that I'd been the one to hurt her. My fears and inability to act had been the catalyst for this whole messed-up night. The realization was a painful reminder of what happened in relationships—even ones steeped in newness and friendship. We had the power to hurt the people we cared about, and it felt shitty to know that I'd wounded Lu with my perceived indifference.

Her hands were still moving nervously in her lap, so I reached over and took one of them in mine. "I'm sorry. I should never have ignored your text or treated you like you didn't matter."

"But you still regret kissing me. You're not sorry you called it a mistake." They weren't questions, but I could tell by the narrowing of her eyes and the accusation in her tone that she wanted an explanation.

Sighing, I admitted, "I like you, Lu. I like you so much. You're smart and funny, and being around you feels as easy as breathing."

The cool blue light from the dashboard illuminated her features. They were twisted up with confusion. "Are you seeing someone? Dating someone from back home, I mean? Is that what you meant when you said you shouldn't have kissed me?"

I was already shaking my head. "No. No, I don't have a girlfriend.

"But," I continued when Lu didn't speak, "I just feel like I'm not a good bet."

The past two months seemed unreal. Losing my job and then packing up to move eighteen hundred miles at the drop of a hat had been enough to turn my quiet life upside down. Finding out the person I was relying on—my one connection to Colorado and the whole reason I'd left everything behind—was basically a figment of my imagination had put the final nail in the coffin of my ability to trust.

I'd been an idiot for being taken in by Virginia. Maybe my instincts were shit, or I didn't know the right people to confide in. Or worse still, Virginia had only wanted some faraway version of me, and when faced with the reality of having me in her life,

I hadn't been what she'd wanted at all. And she'd cast me aside without a backward glance.

I felt like a loser. And honestly, I was afraid of how much Lu could potentially hurt me. It seemed safer if she never got the chance.

"Shouldn't I be the judge of that?" Lu asked quietly. When I didn't answer, she went on, "According to you, I'm the one taking a risk—if you're such a bad bet."

I eyed her, not sure how to feel about someone—anyone—taking a risk on me.

"I'm a big girl, Noah. I can handle it. You warned me. And if you break my heart, then you break my heart."

Her words, spoken so simply, so matter-of-factly, made the breath catch in my chest. As if she already expected to be let down. Lu had experienced loss and indifference over and over again at the hands of her family. She was one forced smile away from heartbreak, so she'd come to anticipate it. And I fucking hated it.

Lu deserved to be cherished. She ought to be worshipped. She needed someone to take her tender, bruised heart and keep it safe. She needed someone she could be herself with—someone to help let down those walls always braced for impact. A person who didn't require her to keep the peace with those good intentions and forced smiles.

Maybe I wasn't the best option. But I wanted Lu to have someone in her life who respected her decisions and only wanted her to be happy. I could be that guy.

My hand tightened around the one I still held. "I wouldn't. I wouldn't break your heart."

Her smile was soft as she took our joined hands and brought them to her face. Soft lips pressed against the center of my palm, and something tightened in my chest as she spoke against my skin. "I know you wouldn't. And I'll take care of yours, I swear."

A promise, sealed with a kiss.

My heart beat a desperate rhythm in my chest, aching to believe but so damn guarded at the same time.

Lu leaned across the bench seat, and I met her halfway, helpless to resist. She hugged me close, and my arms went around her easily. The relief of having her body pressed to mine was overwhelming. I'd spent weeks fighting this—the attraction and the connection I'd recognized the moment she'd gotten into my car.

When we were cheek to cheek, she whispered, "Just give me a chance, Noah. Give *us* a chance." Her breath was warm against my ear, and her voice was so damn patient.

I wanted this. I wanted *her*.

Fighting against self-preservation, I leaned back so I could see her face. In answer, I dipped my head and lowered my lips to hers. Lu parted for me and moved to cup my jaw.

She was softness and light, filling me up and brightening all my darkest shadows.

This kiss felt like a new beginning, like a promise. Our lips moved together, tongues searching.

Her tender touch and bold possession made me weak. But

brave, too. I wanted her closer, so I helped her straddle my lap. The giant bun on the top of Lu's head bumped the top of the Bronco, and she paused, laughing against my lips. She reached up to pull on the band holding all that hair in place, and it cascaded all around us a moment later.

I groaned and threaded my fingers through the strands. "This hair," I said, my voice rough, as I gave a little tug before cupping the back of her head and kissing her deeply. I could still feel the smile on her lips and the way her laughter had shimmered against me.

Her hands explored as we kissed, and mine did the same. With my fingers tracing the line of her back, her touch ghosted over my neck and collarbone. She mapped my shoulders and arms while I brought my hands to rest on her ass. Lu arched against me at the contact, her breasts pressing against my chest. The movement brought her closer everywhere, and my dick strained behind my jeans to reach her.

Our kisses turned a little wild, going sloppy and wet, her lips dragging to my jaw as I kneaded her backside. She felt so good under my hands and on top of me, surrounding me.

Lu worked her way back to my ear, taking the lobe in her mouth and delivering a quick bite. My eyes rolled back as she pressed her center against my erection.

"Will you touch me?" she whispered against the shell of my ear.

My mind spun, and I was pretty sure I was going to die if I didn't feel her skin. So I nodded in answer.

She took one of my hands and placed it on her thigh, where she was spread wide for me. My fingers delved under her dress, skating up the smooth fabric of her tights. I reached the heat of her core with the pad of my thumb, brushing softly against the material covering her.

Lu gasped softly by my ear, and her hips jerked at the contact. So I did it again and again, feeling her shift against me, seeking more. I pressed harder, moving my thumb in small circles at the apex of her thighs. With the hand still clutching her ass, I encouraged her to move, to find a rhythm and take her pleasure for herself as much as I was giving it to her.

I could have watched Lu all night. Her wild, untamed beauty as she reached higher and higher. With her eyes closed and her gasps painting eager little breaths across her lips, I wanted this for her. Even if she were the only one finding release tonight, this would be more than enough because she needed it, and I needed her.

Moments later, Lu's lips came back to mine in a flurry. Her tongue stroked into my mouth, and I groaned as her movements became more frantic and searching.

She broke the kiss and murmured against my open mouth, "I'm close. You feel so good."

I kissed her chin and the corner of her lips—wherever I could reach—as she panted against me, hips moving.

Finally, impatient and desperate to feel her bare skin, I snaked my other hand beneath her dress and her tights and underwear, clutching her ass in a firm grip. She dropped her head to my shoulder and moaned.

Against the warm skin of her neck, I breathed out, her name a prayer and a benediction in my rasped exhalation, "Luanne."

She released a hitching breath as she came, pulsing hot and wet through her tights.

I gentled my movements as she came back to herself, breathing heavily where her head rested on my shoulder.

One of my hands relaxed on her thigh while the other drew lines on the soft skin of her back.

First times were always awkward. I waited for discomfort or uneasiness to descend, but it never came.

Instead, Lu leaned back to look at me. Even in the dim light, I could see her flushed cheeks and bright eyes. She bit her lip before shaking her head slightly, amusement fighting its way forward. "Well, I didn't hate it when you said it like that."

CHAPTER 9

Noah

The foliage had peaked in Cozy Creek. Tourists were everywhere, and at least three autumn-themed activities were happening every week.

Driving past the visitor center, I noticed the marquee: *Fall-elujah! It's almost time for the Fall Festival! Get your tickets today.*

Shaking my head, I fought a smile. This town was . . . something else.

"Are you going to the Fall Festival, Noah?" Mrs. Angelo called from the back seat.

I replied a little louder than normal so she was sure to hear, "I was thinking about it. What about you?"

"I don't know. Always a lot of out-of-towners there. But you should go. Young people enjoy it. All the rides and games. Carnival food, too. It's the only time of the year you can get those deep-fried pumpkin hand pies. You should at least go on a hayride."

"I'll think about it, Mrs. Angelo. Thank you."

The elderly woman in the back seat was a regular. Every Monday since I'd taken the job driving for Huber, I picked up Mrs. Angelo at 5:15 p.m. sharp and took her to visit her cats at the pet cemetery. I waited while she sat on a nearby bench and then took her back home. She always invited me to stay for dinner, and I always declined. But I never charged her for the ride, and she passed me a Werther's Original when I opened her door in front of her home at 6:00 p.m.

Mrs. Angelo had a daughter who lived in town and some grandkids out of state, but she liked keeping up her regular visits to the cemetery, and I was happy to take her. She was brutally honest and a little grouchy, but I enjoyed talking to her on our rides.

Her encouragement to attend the Fall Festival made me think of Lu. Maybe she'd want to go with me. The girl was in love with fall, and I could imagine how she'd light up, taking me around and showing me all the things she loved about the festival. I smiled to myself at the thought as I pulled up to the last stoplight before we cleared downtown and the tourist traffic.

It had been two days since Lu and I had talked in the back of the Bronco—among other things. Things I was reliving in my mind with alarming distraction. The sounds she'd made. Her warmth and the feel of her body moving against mine. I'd never be able to glance in the rearview mirror again without thinking about Saturday night.

After I'd helped her off my lap, she'd reached for me, hands going to the button of my jeans. But I'd stopped her. Not because I hadn't been desperate for her touch but I wanted to do this right. Go slow. There would be other opportunities to be together. It didn't need to be rushed in the back seat of the Bronco at three in the morning like we were teenagers. I was giving this thing between us a chance despite my fears and instincts. Besides, I didn't want Lu to regret anything. Going too far too fast was the quickest way to fuck things up.

So we'd climbed in the front seat, and I'd taken her home, walked her to her door, and kissed her good night. We'd been texting for the past two days. I had Wednesday night off and planned to take her out, or we could stay in together—whatever she wanted. But it would be a real date outside the confines of Huber rides and casual run-ins.

She was more than just a dream girl now. This was real.

With my mind, once again, distracted and thinking of Lu, I glanced at the vehicle idling beside me and did a double take. It was Lu.

In an older cherry-red Jeep Wrangler, singing her heart out, was the girl I couldn't stop thinking about. The girl whose car was supposed to be in the shop.

Glancing forward, I saw the stoplight was still red. Tourists crossed in front of our vehicles, and Mrs. Angelo hummed softly in the back seat. But I couldn't focus because Lu was right there, in the driver's seat.

Straightening, I pushed my sunglasses on top of my head. The movement must have caught her attention out of the corner of her eye because she turned and froze. Whatever song lyric she'd been belting out died on her lips, and she stared back at me.

I lowered my window and shouted, "Lu!"

She winced and tried to slouch down in her seat—like I couldn't see her. Jesus Christ.

"Lu!" I yelled again.

Her passenger window rolled down, but she still remained ducked low.

"Lu, what are you doing?"

She popped up suddenly. "Oh, hey, Noah! Hi! How are you?"

I stared, incredulous.

"Your car is out of the shop?" I said it like a question to give her an out, but it definitely came out like an accusation. She hadn't mentioned getting her car back. And I'd literally given her a ride home two nights ago.

"Yeah?" she replied, and it sounded like a question, too.

"Did you just get it back?"

She made a face that told me no, she did not *just* get her car back, and she hadn't wanted to admit that.

Exasperation and impatience heavy in my tone, along with a healthy dose of *what the fuck*, I asked, "Lu?"

Dropping her chin to her chest, she admitted, "I've had it back for a while."

My mind spun, considering all the rides I'd given her, all the money she'd paid to go places around town, and all the way to the Denver airport.

"How long was it in the shop?"

Cringing, she confessed, "About a week."

I felt my eyes bulge in surprise. "I gave you rides for over a month!"

A horn honked behind us, and I glanced up to see the light was green. "Pull over," I called to Lu before speeding up through the light. I drove past the busy end of Main Street and then turned right into the bank parking lot. Lu shifted into the lane behind me and followed.

"I'm sorry for the interruption, Mrs. Angelo. This will just take a minute."

"No worries," she replied. "Leave the window down if you don't mind."

I shot her a confused look in the rearview, but I was too focused on figuring out what was going on with Lu to care.

Hopping out of my car, I opened the passenger door to the Jeep where she'd parked beside me and climbed in.

"What the hell, Lu?"

I took in her panicked expression and her wild blond hair held back by a headband.

"I know!" she wailed and rested her head on the steering wheel. "I'm sorry! At first, I requested the rides because I needed them. Something was going on with the Jeep. The engine made a weird sound, so I took it in. Then you showed up and replaced Zoe, and we started hanging out."

"But you kept calling for a Huber? Why would you do that?"

Lu finally raised her head and looked at me. Her red cheeks radiated fiery embarrassment. "Because I liked you, okay? I wanted to spend more time together and get to know you. And you were weirdly afraid of me."

Of course I was afraid of her. She was a hot girl who was also awesome, and I'd just gotten dumped in the most humiliating way imaginable. I'd kept my distance out of prideful self-preservation.

And of fucking course she drove a red Jeep Wrangler. Lu was basically teenage Noah's fantasy come to life.

"I didn't mean to lie," she rushed to add. "It was just the only way I could spend time with you—even as friends—with how skittish you were around me."

I sighed and really thought about what she'd admitted. Suddenly, the seriousness of being deceived for weeks left me like the air rushing out of a balloon. She'd requested rides she didn't need in order to hang out with me. I pressed my lips together as a smile fought to work itself out in flattered freedom.

Her pretty gray eyes were tortured. "I'm sorry I let you think my car was in the shop all this time. I was going to tell you now that we're . . . you know, dating. Hanging out? Whatever."

"Dating," I confirmed. "So you paid to spend time with me."

She nodded, looking horribly uncomfortable.

"Like a gigolo."

Slapping a palm to her forehead, she groaned, and my laughter finally escaped.

Her gaze snapped to mine, wide and incredulous. "Do you know I seriously worried about committing prostitution?"

I laughed harder, holding my stomach. "That's only if you pay for sex," I wheezed. "You complete nut."

Lu whacked me on the shoulder. "Stop laughing at me," she cried, but she was laughing too, cheeks still violently red.

She went in to whack me again, but I snagged her hand, pressing a quick kiss to her palm before hauling her toward me. "I deserve to give you a little bit of shit about this. And maybe it's kind of cute that you wanted to spend time with me so bad."

She immediately sobered, face stricken with remorse. "I am sorry that I lied. I was wrong." Her gray eyes were as sincere as her words. Lu worried her bottom lip, visibly anxious and genuine in her regret.

I shrugged. I knew what it was like to be lied to by someone determined to do damage. Lu's lie of omission wasn't going to send me spiraling, mostly because I knew the intent behind it. "It wasn't malicious, and you never outright lied to me. Unless you made up a carburetor shaft tank?"

Her nose wrinkled. "I actually don't know what was wrong. I'm not good with cars. The mechanic said some of those words, but I might have gotten the order wrong."

I smiled and leaned in to press my lips to hers. "Of course you have a bright red Jeep."

"It's my baby. I've had it since high school."

"So hot," I groaned.

Her grin unfurled against my lips, and I loved the intimacy of it. Making her smile and feeling it take shape, having her close and keeping her there.

But after a moment, I sat back. "I need to go. I have to take Mrs. Angelo to visit Noodles and Foxy."

Lu peeked around my shoulder, obviously just realizing I had someone in the Bronco. "Oh God."

I turned with her and saw the elderly woman wave.

Leaning across my body, Lu called out the still-open passenger window and into mine, "I'm so sorry, Mrs. Angelo!"

"No trouble, dear! This was better than one of those Netflix shows!"

I huffed out a laugh as Lu's body shook against mine. Annnd, I needed to get out of here before I had other, less innocent thoughts about Lu's body pressed to mine.

"I'll text you later," I said, giving her one last quick kiss. "We're on for Wednesday?"

"Yep," she confirmed, eyes bright.

"Later, Luke Skywalker."

When I finished driving for the night, I came home to my apartment over the Cozy Creek Confectionery. Madi would be in soon to start the bread, and then once I'd showered and settled into bed, I'd fall asleep to the smell of warmth and comfort.

But first I needed to check my email. I'd seen a notification pop up while I was driving Arnie Buchanan home from work.

There was a new message from my website's contact form. Everything had been up and running for about a week, but I hadn't advertised or posted my availability as a freelance website developer anywhere. I was actually planning on talking to Lu about locals I could approach who needed more of an online presence.

So the random person finding me and reaching out through the vastness of the internet was pretty unexpected. But the request seemed valid, and while super friendly and generous with her exclamation points, the stranger didn't seem to be trolling me. A graphic designer who lived in Chicago needed a website for her book cover and graphics services. She wanted to get my rate for design, setup and maintenance, and updates to the site. She seemed serious.

I didn't know how this Becca Kernsy had found me, but as long as the deposit went through, she would be my very first client. I emailed her back to clarify the scope of work and passed along the other payment details, even offering to have a call whenever she was ready. I was surprised to get an immediate reply at this time of night, but there she was, bright and enthusiastic in my inbox. We set up a time to talk the following day.

Sitting back in the chair at the kitchen table I'd been using as a desk, I couldn't help but laugh in surprise. I had my first client. Maybe I could really do this.

I closed my laptop and went into the bedroom. I took my keys and wallet out of my pockets before depositing them on top of the dresser. My eyes went to the painting by Lu, and I smiled.

I wondered what she'd have to say about my first client in this new venture. Probably something positive and upbeat—that was just her. She'd be encouraging and optimistic with an unwavering confidence in me that I likely didn't deserve.

Once more, the possibility of staying in Cozy Creek crept into my head. I thought about it while I shucked my clothes into the hamper and turned on the water to heat. Driving for Jimmy could pay the bills until I found enough clients to keep me afloat. I'd already applied for my business license in Colorado, established my LLC, and set up a separate business account at the local bank. Those had just been administrative things done with practicality and convenience in mind. But now, I had options.

The loss of my job and the move. The breakup. It had all been a house of cards crumpling to the ground. I'd simply been reacting and surviving.

Now, I felt like I had choices—decisions that could be made in my best interest. I had a business and a client with the potential for more. I had a steady income, a decent apartment, and was starting to make connections in this tiny town. And I had a girl who I couldn't get off my mind.

Grabbing my phone, I pulled up my text thread with Lu, knowing she'd see my messages when she woke up in a couple of hours.

Me: I'm updating your contact in my phone to Richard Gere. Make sure you change mine to Pretty Woman.

Me: Pizza and a movie Wednesday? I'll bring you a milkshake. Bet I can guess your favorite. *types in revenge*

Me: Can you give me that guy's contact info? The firefighter runner you mentioned. Cole something. Thanks.

Me: Good morning, Louisville Slugger.

Maybe leaving wasn't the only option anymore.

And then I told myself not to get my hopes up and stepped into the shower.

CHAPTER 10

Lu

A knock on the door had me smiling, especially knowing who waited on the other side.

I hurried through the living room and pulled the door open wide. "I was promised a milkshake."

Noah grinned. "How about pizza instead? There might even be stuffed crust."

"Ohhhh." I clapped my hands and reached for the plastic grocery bag dangling from his hand while he cradled the pizza box. "That's an appropriate substitution. Come on in."

Noah stepped into my apartment and nudged the front door closed with his elbow. "What are we watching?" he asked.

I'd thought about doing the girl thing where you say you don't care and whatever is totally fine. But that wasn't me. So I grinned mischievously and said, "One of my favorite eighties movies. All the machines and cars and electronics come to life because of a comet passing by the earth, and they terrorize and kill people in this town."

He made a disbelieving face. "What? Why?"

"The comet makes them do it. I don't know. It's a classic. You'll love it."

Noah appeared unconvinced.

We deposited the pizza and drinks on my coffee table and then settled in next to one another. Unlike the first time we watched television together, I wasn't worried about keeping my distance and scaring Noah off. Well, I was still a little concerned about frightening Noah away. Yes, things had progressed between us, and we were dating—his word choice—but Noah still had some uncertainty lingering around him. A fear in his eyes told me he was trying really hard to trust me, but he wasn't all the way there yet. And, honestly, getting caught driving the Jeep when he still thought it was in the shop had not been a good look. I still felt awful about not telling him the truth upfront.

During the long intro of the opening credits, Noah and I got situated with our food. He cast me a quick look before glancing back at his plate.

"What?" I asked, then took a bite of my slice.

"So I had someone contact me about building a website for them."

I chewed quickly so I could freak out. "That's amazing! Was it someone in town? How did they hear about you?"

Noah shook his head. "She just found my website by chance. It was really strange, but she contacted me a few days ago. We had a call to go over things and I'm working on it for her."

"I am so excited for you. And when you're ready for more clients, you just let me know."

He smiled. "I will."

I realized I didn't really know what Noah did for work before moving to Cozy Creek. "Do you enjoy that sort of work? Is this a new development?"

He chewed thoughtfully and took his time answering. "It is new, but yeah, I do enjoy it. Computer science was my major back in school. I'd always intended to go into web and app development."

I badly wanted to ask more questions, but Noah still hadn't offered up a lot of personal details—including why he'd come to Colorado and why he was driving for Jimmy Huber. Something about the way his eyes fastened on the television didn't invite a follow-up response.

So, I murmured, "That's really cool."

"And I talked to Cole Sutter. He said you'd mentioned me. Thanks for setting that up. I went for a run with him on his lunch break yesterday."

Nodding, I fought not to make too big a deal about that. Cole was a great guy with ties to the community as a member of the Cozy Creek Fire Brigade. I wanted Noah to fit in and be happy here, and if he had more friends, maybe he'd like it more.

Since I'd first met Noah, everything about him screamed cautious mistrust. Sometimes I got the feeling that Cozy Creek was this temporary stopover. Not everyone wanted to settle down, and I knew that.

But my roots were here. This was where I grew up—where I'd had fifteen years with my mother and fought to keep a relationship with my father. I loved this town.

Selfishly, I wanted Noah to accept this place that meant so much to me. I wanted it to be home for him too. He was already so important. You didn't just meet someone every day that you felt an undeniable connection with. I'd been attempting to date for the better part of a year. I knew that Noah was special. My heart knew it too.

But he wasn't ready to hear all that. He needed to take things slow, one day at a time. And if this new routine with Cole gave him another tie to Cozy Creek, then I would try to play it cool.

"That's great," I replied casually. "He's a nice guy."

Eventually pizza consumption slowed and we settled into the couch and watched the movie. Noah was equal parts entertained and horrified. We laughed together and teased, and eventually, he reached for my hand and laced our fingers together.

At one point, I glanced over and saw Noah's eyes were closed. The movie had only about ten minutes left, but it was late. I knew his schedule was a little wacky since he drove the evening and night shift for Jimmy. But he also didn't like to sleep the day away. That probably made it easy for weariness to kick in when Noah finally sat down and let himself relax, no matter the time of day.

Leaning forward, I slowly grabbed the remote and lowered the volume so it didn't disturb him. And then I watched him sleep like a total creeper.

His breaths were deep and even, chest rising and falling beneath his gray Henley. Long dark lashes rested on the tops of his cheeks. His light brown hair was getting pretty long on the top. I bet he hadn't found a place to have it cut since moving here. His hand still held mine, not loosening at all in his sleep. My eyes traced the line of his profile and all the scruff on his jaw.

I was just thinking about how handsome he was and how much I liked looking at him when the end credits and the music stopped.

Noah blinked sleepy hazel eyes open before he found me next to him. "Staring at my unconscious body, were you?"

Unable to help myself, I grinned. "Yes, Sleeping Beauty. You ready for bed?" His dark brows rose in surprise, but I brazened it out and kept going. "You can stay if you want. I have a fresh toothbrush you can use. And then I won't have to worry about you crashing and dying on the way home."

He shifted and propped his elbow up on the arm of the couch, resting his head in his hand and staring at me. "What is it with you and transportation and dying? First, the flight where you weaseled a hug out of me, and now this. Cars are pretty safe, Looney Tunes."

I turned toward him on the couch, pulling my knees up and letting my feet hang off the side. "I'm just awesome like that."

Noah's gaze was warm and amused. "Yeah, I guess you are."

LANEY HATCHER

"We can just . . . sleep," I offered, my voice soft.

He nodded slowly. "Yeah. Okay."

Rising, I held out my hand, and Noah took it, following me down the hallway. I grabbed the spare toothbrush and left him in the bathroom while I took our dishes and trash to the kitchen.

I met Noah back in the hallway and led him to my bedroom. He helped me remove all my throw pillows, and we folded the comforter and the sheets back together.

"I'm just going to go change," I told him, the sound of my voice breaking the silence. It wasn't awkward, but it was tense. Expectant, even. But I meant what I'd said. Just sleep. Despite my orgasm in the back seat of the Bronco last week, I wasn't rushing Noah into anything.

After grabbing some pajamas from my dresser, I turned to peek at him from the doorway. Noah was toeing off his boots and unbuttoning his jeans.

I made quick work of my nighttime routine and slipped into a tie-dye sweatshirt and matching lounge shorts. Noah was already in my bed when I got back. The bright overhead light was now off, with just the bedside lamp casting the room in a soft glow. His skin was painted gold, the tops of his rounded shoulders sticking out from the blankets were bare and smooth.

I wanted to touch him. To glide my hands over his leanly muscled body. But instead, I slipped beneath the covers and turned on my side to face him.

"I like your pj's," Noah said, voice soft and sleepy again.

Lifting the covers and sneaking a glance beneath, I grinned

143

and said, "I like yours too."

Noah laughed, and I ignored the way it made my stomach swoop. I also didn't let myself focus on the fact that he was in my bed in just his black boxer briefs and bright white socks.

Reaching back, I turned off the lamp and plunged the room into darkness. I could make out Noah's silhouette from the ambient light from the windows.

"Good night, Noah."

"Good night, Luanne," he replied softly.

I fought a shiver at the use of my full name in that low voice—the same one that had whispered in my ear as I came. Tugging the blankets around my shoulders, I tried to force myself to relax despite the fact that there was a person in bed with me for the first time in a very long time.

It turned out that falling asleep with Noah was just as easy as everything else with him. I didn't toss and turn and spend hours staring at the ceiling before sleep claimed me. I dropped right off, content and warm and feeling like I was exactly where I belonged.

When I woke the following morning, it was still early. But I didn't think I could fall back asleep. I was a chronic early riser and there was also the fact that I was wrapped up in Noah.

He was spooning me from behind, his chest warm against my back as he breathed deep and even. His thighs tucked neatly along mine, all our long lines matching up. His face was probably buried under a mountain of blond hair, but if he minded, I couldn't tell.

Shifting just a bit, I rose to check the time. The phone on my bedside table said 6:42 a.m.

Noah's body edged closer at my subtle movement. His arm tightened around my waist, drawing me to him, and I felt something hard pressed to my backside.

Warmth flooded my system, and I fought the urge to arch into him. The instinct to grind my ass against his erection was admittedly strong.

I froze as Noah's face nuzzled my back, a sleepy groan rumbling close enough to feel. His hips flexed as he continued to wake up, the solid length of him insistent and oh-so welcome.

I could tell the moment awareness and wakefulness entered the chat because Noah became utterly still, even his breaths halted.

"Good morning," I said, my voice going breathless.

"Uh, morning." He cleared the roughness from his throat. "Sorry. I didn't realize I was a snuggler."

He lifted his arm from where he had it draped across me, but I reached down and kept him from retreating. "Don't be sorry. I like it. I'm a snuggler, too. Which probably doesn't surprise you at all."

Noah huffed a laugh, and I felt the heat of his breath, the force of his exhalation, his heart beating steady against me. I wanted to hear him sigh into my hair. To curse and moan and fall into me.

Carefully and slowly—so slowly—I rolled over to face him. I took in his pink cheeks and his sleep-mussed hair and thought my heart might be in real trouble here.

"Can I kiss you?" I asked, conscious of the promise I'd made the night before.

In answer, Noah brought his forehead to mine. I felt his arm ease back around me, holding me close and drawing me in.

I tangled my legs with his before cupping his jaw and pressing my lips to his. He made a sound deep in his throat when I arched my back. The contact between my breasts and his chest did nothing to ease the ache I felt growing between us. The closer I got, the closer I wanted to be.

Things got heated pretty quickly. Our kisses turned wild, and our hands restless. Noah fastened his lips to my neck as my nails scraped across his shoulder blades. His hand was in the back of my underwear, cupping my ass and bringing us even closer. The erection pressing into my stomach was hot and hard and impossible to ignore.

Reaching low, I gripped Noah's dick through the fabric. His lips stuttered against the column of my throat, and a sharp inhale met my ears.

"Can I?" I breathed, terrified that he might say no. That he might not want this—want me.

But I felt him nod, forehead resting against my collarbone.

I gave a squeeze and felt his cock jump within my hold. Then I snaked my hand between us and beneath the waistband of his boxer briefs to touch him, skin to skin. He was hot and hard, and I wanted to make him feel as wild as he made me.

There was another harsh inhale from Noah when I started to

move, pumping his firm length as his hips jerked forward, seeking my touch. I kept up a steady rhythm as his hands resumed massaging the globes of my ass.

When Noah's breathing became ragged, I removed my hand to urge him flat on his back. He seemed dazed as he watched me climb between his spread thighs and lower his boxer briefs to expose his dick to the cool morning air. My bedroom was still dim in the emerging daylight, but I could see him well enough, so hard and eager before me. His lean torso was taut and rigid as he awaited my next move, hazel eyes never leaving my face. I felt powerful and worshiped at the same time.

"Can I?" I repeated as I took his length in my grasp once more, slowly pumping up and down.

Noah's hand reached down to cover mine and pause my movement, but he didn't push me away. "I can't think with you doing that."

"Oh." I grinned unrepentant. I wanted Noah out of control for me—wanting me, needing me.

"What are you asking, Lu?"

My thumb leisurely traced the vein running along his impressive shaft, loving the feel of him, eager to put that dazed look right back on his handsome face. "Can I touch you here?"

Noah's throat worked as he swallowed, hazel eyes following my movements.

"Can I taste you here?" I asked, once I reached the flared head of his cock, smearing his arousal with the pad of my thumb.

His plump lips—kiss-swollen from our earlier kisses—parted

before he finally said, "You don't have to."

"I know. I want to, though. If that's okay with you."

His nod was tentative and cautious, as was his gaze. But then I leaned forward and swallowed him down as deep as I could go, and his eyelids closed, and he groaned.

I pulled back and swirled my tongue around his tip, gathering another bead of liquid and tasting him.

Using my hand to help, I set a pace as I moved over him, drawing him in and out of my eager mouth in a steady pace. I played around a little to find out what he liked, licking and sucking, hollowing my cheeks and using my other hand to cup his balls.

His hand snaked into my hair when I relaxed my tongue flat against the underside of his dick.

Color high and brows furrowed, Noah muttered, "Fuck," and guided my movements to a rhythm he liked.

I loved how Noah looked in my bed and how it felt to wake up with him. Heat built in my core when I remembered the feel of him, hard and unyielding against my ass. I let go of his balls to reach down my body. Slipping my fingers into my underwear, I gathered the growing wetness and brought it to my clit. I used three fingers to circle there, providing relief to the tension coiling tight inside me.

When I lifted my gaze, Noah was watching me, how my arm was angled, allowing me to touch myself. Another groan left his lips, and I knew I wanted to hear that sound again—with him inside me, behind me, surrounding me. I wanted to feel the rumble of his pleasure against my lips and in a million different ways.

This was the beginning for us. I couldn't forget the way he'd looked at me when we'd talked and he'd touched me in the back seat of the Bronco. He knew what was happening between us was ... something else—something more. He *had* to.

And a blow job in my bed wasn't repayment for services rendered and orgasms delivered. This was seeing the look on his face and knowing I'd put it there. The pleasure, the wonder, and the overwhelming relief of meeting someone's needs—being the face of their desire. Even more than that—making their needs your own.

I liked the feel of him on my tongue and the way he gripped my hair, like he couldn't help himself. But more than anything, I loved taking the tight leash of Noah's self-control and wrapping it around my fist. I wanted him to come apart for me, the way I'd dissolved under his touch, the way I was coming apart right now from my own hand, and how he was looking at me.

I hummed against his flesh as my orgasm pulsed beneath my fingertips.

The tendons in Noah's neck strained, and he blew out a sharp breath. "I'm gonna come. You feel too good, and I can't—I'm gonna come."

Keeping my eyes on him, I saw the moment all his muscles went taut before he crossed the point of no return. His release flooded my mouth in waves, and I swallowed it down as Noah's body eventually relaxed into the mattress.

The hand tangled in my hair loosened, combing gently through the unruly strands. "Come here."

I climbed up his body, placing a few soft kisses as I went, before settling at his side. Noah drew me close, urging my head onto his chest while his hand still played in my hair. I felt the wild beat of his heart thundering beneath my ear and stayed long enough to listen as it gentled, settling into something quiet and content.

My body eventually relaxed into sleep as Noah held me. Our breaths deep and even. My heart wrecked and helpless and utterly undone.

CHAPTER 11

I stared at the text thread with my stepmother and sighed. After two unanswered messages—both read—I'd given up and called the restaurant she'd mentioned taking my dad to for his birthday.

The hostess who'd answered at the Laurel Park Inn happened to be a girl I'd babysat a decade ago as a teenager. Kayleigh had recognized my name on the caller ID, but if she thought it was weird that I was asking about reservations with very little to go on, she didn't say anything. She'd scanned their calendar system and confirmed a reservation for three tomorrow evening at seven o'clock under the name Kimberly Billings.

I'd ignored the hurt and confusion swirling inside me and asked Kayleigh to update that to four guests before thanking her and disconnecting.

That familiar bitterness threatened to rise, but I pushed it away. Why would Kimberly exclude me? Why couldn't we be some semblance of a family? I knew that was what my father wanted. It wasn't like I stole his attention. We didn't have father-daughter lunches or anything requiring his time beyond the occasional phone call. After all these years, why couldn't Kimberly invite me to be a small part of their lives?

Two women I didn't recognize approached my booth, so I flipped my phone over and placed it on the tabletop, focusing my attention on my customers.

The farmers' market was busy as tourists meandered the stalls and talked to the vendors. I'd met some really sweet ladies from California and talked them into checking out Dottie's Ice Cream as well as picking up a pack of greeting cards from my display. The sun was bright, but the October afternoon was chilly. A perfect fall day that made me want to go apple picking or split a funnel cake with Noah.

I fought a dreamy sigh as the two customers browsed the stock I had left. Noah had been busy with work, both driving and with website stuff. But we'd been texting and talking since our night together earlier in the week.

We'd woken up the second time and managed to make it out of bed. I smiled when I thought about a mussed and attentive Noah who'd had a hard time keeping his hands off me. He'd held my hand out of the apartment and on the drive over to grab breakfast burritos at Tres Chicas, my favorite food truck in town. I'd gotten shy smiles and hot looks throughout breakfast before he'd driven me home and kissed me senseless in the parking lot.

When the women finished making their purchases—two prints, a coffee mug, and four friendship bracelets—they stepped aside to reveal Noah waiting patiently behind them with two cups in his hands.

He took a sip of his bubble tea and held one out to me. "What's up, Louis Vuitton?"

I couldn't help the smile that came over my face. I knew it hadn't been very long since I'd seen him, and maybe I was getting ahead of myself, letting my feelings run away from me, but I was happy. And why shouldn't I let myself be?

Why did happiness need to be suppressed or measured out in careful doses? Declaring your joy to the universe didn't make it strip away any faster. I wanted to live in this moment with a guy I liked while he flirted with me and made me smile. I wasn't going to hide it just because it might not last forever.

"Hey, you," I said, feeling my cheeks strain as I accepted the drink. "You want to come sit? Watch the magic happen?"

"Oh, you know it." Noah ducked around the side of the tent and slid into the empty folding chair beside me. He pressed a quick kiss to my cheek that had me grinning before I leaned over and smacked a kiss to his lips in return.

"What have you been up to today?" I finally managed after battling the butterflies in my stomach.

"Not much. Ran with Cole and Pace at lunch and then worked on Becca's site for a bit."

"Ohhh. How's that going?"

Noah's lips closed around his straw for a moment, and I followed the movement. "It's nearly done actually. What she wanted was pretty basic as far as design and layout. She just needs me to make regular updates and maintain it, but that won't be too difficult." I nodded as if I had any idea what monitoring a website entailed. "But Becca actually recommended me to some of her clients. I have requests from several of her author friends in my inbox."

Wiggling in my seat, I couldn't help my excitement. "Noah! That's amazing!"

Even he couldn't quash his grin. Hazel eyes gleamed momentarily before he carefully tucked his excitement away. Noah was one of those people who didn't trust happiness that fell into your lap. He was waiting on the universe to snatch it away. And I didn't know how to help him enjoy it while it lasted, but maybe we'd get there . . . together.

Another idea struck me, and I wondered aloud, "Would you want to build a website for me?"

"Really?"

I nodded earnestly. "I could really use a site for DeLuLu Designs. Direct sales, a storefront, the whole nine yards. I'd pay you," I rushed to add. "Not just in blow jobs."

Noah choked on his bubble tea, and I laughed.

"Plus, I should get in on this early before you have all the clients you can handle."

He looked thoughtful. "Yeah, we can do that. Do you want to come over next week, and we'll sketch it out? Exactly what you want and how you want it to look. Find examples of sites you like and what you're looking for."

"I can do that."

A few customers wandered over, and I talked to them about my work and the town. Noah watched and listened but hung back and let me do my thing. When locals drifted by, I introduced him. He was more open and friendly than I'd ever seen him. And that gave me hope too. Maybe Noah was settling in, learning to love this town despite whatever mysterious beginning had brought him here.

After I'd bagged up a few prints and sent a cute middle-aged couple on their way with a recommendation for a dinner spot, Noah cleared his throat. "I actually stopped by because I wanted to see if you'd like to go to the Fall Festival with me next weekend. I got some tickets. Thought it might be fun. I heard there are these pumpkin hand pies you can only get there."

He was rambling, and it was adorable.

Grinning, I put him out of his misery. "I'd love to go. Thank you for inviting me."

"Cool," he muttered, making my teeth hurt with that shy smile.

"Cool," I repeated. "And I'll pick *you* up for a change."

Noah laughed, and the sound was music to my ears.

The Laurel Park Inn was a former bed-and-breakfast halfway up the mountain. The owners shifted focus and renovated in the nineties to turn the whole thing into a two-level restaurant. There was even porch seating on the second floor during the summer months.

My dad was a big fan of the restaurant. It had been his favorite for the last decade or so. The views of the Rockies were amazing and the food and drinks were pretty great, too.

I'd made sure to arrive in the reception area well ahead of Kimberly's seven o'clock reservation. Dad's gift was wrapped and tucked under my arm—a Joni Mitchell vinyl from 1974 that I'd acquired in a bidding war on an online auction site four months ago. I knew he'd like it. He and my mom had loved Joni Mitchell.

The front door opened with a gust of chilly air, and Kimberly and Ginny stepped in ahead of my father. They were all dressed nicely for the occasion. I caught the surprise on the faces of two out of three of them, but Dad smiled and gave me a hug and a hello.

I greeted my stepfamily and made sure my tone was level and friendly. It didn't matter that they'd purposely left me out of their plans for my dad's birthday dinner. I was here, and my dad was happy. That was all that mattered.

We were seated near the windows on the upper floor, and drinks were ordered. Ginny talked about her upcoming season on the slopes. She was a ski instructor and spent the majority of her time between November and April living and working at the resort. We hadn't been skiing together since Dad had taken us for a weekend during our senior year of high school—an attempt at forced bonding that obviously hadn't stuck. She'd bailed on me and gone on the more advanced runs. I remembered how skilled Ginny was compared to my less-than-graceful slide down the mountain.

She always thought it was such a waste that I wasn't interested in the sport but lived close enough to some of the best skiing in the country. It had never been my thing, though, and I was okay with that.

During our meal, I stayed quiet for the most part, nibbling on appetizers and listening to my stepmother and stepsister chat. Dad nodded along in whatever direction the conversation flowed. Eventually, after the single-serve chocolate lava cake arrived with bright sparklers, my dad asked how I was and what I'd been up to lately.

Kimberly and Ginny were still talking quietly to each other, so I felt safe mentioning that I was seeing someone.

"Well, that's nice, honey," my dad replied. "What does he do?"

"Oh, um, he's a web designer. Works remotely, but he'll probably be taking on clients in town, too."

Dad smiled. "Always nice to have someone good with technology around."

"Yeah," I agreed.

"What's that, Luanne? You finally found a boyfriend?" Ginny's sickly-sweet voice came from across the candlelit table.

I glanced around, noticing that my dad had missed the snipe implied in her questions. Kimberly ignored us in favor of her phone.

Swallowing uncomfortably, I was eager to get the attention

off me. Some high school habits didn't go away. Painting a target on myself wasn't something I wanted to do with Ginny, a person who still thrived in her mean-girl era.

"It's still really new," I replied finally, reaching for my glass of wine.

"I bet it is," Ginny murmured with a cruel gleam in her eye. As if anyone who stayed long enough was sure to get tired of me or annoyed with me—whatever the implied insult was with that statement. I took a deep breath to push away the hurt.

"Well, I'd like to meet this new guy," Dad cut in, oblivious to the underlying tension that had my knee vibrating beneath the white tablecloth. "Let's have dinner at the house in a few weeks. You can invite your fella, Lu, and we'll have a nice send-off for Ginny before she leaves us for the ski season."

"Sounds great, Ben," my stepsister answered with a smile.

"Sure, Dad," I agreed without meeting her gaze.

Quickly changing the subject, I asked Dad about the school and the various fall functions keeping him busy.

The meal wrapped up shortly thereafter, and my father went on his way with Kimberly and Ginny.

I drove carefully down the mountain back toward town. They'd gotten some snow up in the higher elevations recently. My thoughts ran over our conversation this evening and how it had been mostly fine—typical. At least Dad hadn't brought up interviewing for the elementary art teacher position again or my hobby of a career.

Nothing had been greatly altered because of my presence. I'd forced myself onto the guest list, unwanted and unwelcome. And now that I was stewing in my emotions, I wondered why I'd even bothered. I could have just caught up with Dad at the house or invited him for lunch to give him his present and celebrate his birthday that way.

I didn't know why it had been so important for me to be there at the restaurant tonight.

Maybe because I knew that if I hadn't bothered, the occasion would have passed by with only their three-person family unit to acknowledge it. Maybe I desperately wanted to be included. And maybe I didn't understand why everything had to be so damn hard.

Why do you bend over backward for people who don't care about you?

That voice in my head sounded suspiciously like Noah as I stared out the Jeep's windshield.

I remembered his words from the night we'd met.

"The effort of maintaining a relationship should go both ways and be equal. Not one person killing themselves to keep it all together."

He hadn't planted the seed of dissent within me, but he'd made me aware of it. And I could probably guess what he'd have to say about dinner tonight and the circumstances surrounding it.

But that was Noah, waiting for happiness to be dragged away from him and always questioning motivations. He didn't trust easily. And he'd talked about his own parents like they were acquaintances.

My dad was still my dad. I loved him, and he loved me. Writing him off wasn't something I was capable of doing, so I would just keep trying. And besides, he'd wanted to plan another dinner. He was interested in my life and wanted to meet Noah. That was progress—proof that my efforts weren't all one-sided.

Okay, yes. Maybe with Kimberly and Ginny they were. I'd been trying for years to make things less awkward and more than just cordial. Family was important. You didn't just give up on it. Not when you barely had anyone left to call family. Not when cutting someone out of your life meant you were the one left holding the cord. I'd just have to try harder.

Ignoring the uneasy ache in the pit of my stomach, I noticed the lights of Cozy Creek in the distance. Checking the time on the dashboard, I hit the button to call Noah.

"Hey there, Loofah," he said, and I smiled, something tight within going a little bit looser.

"Hey. You busy?"

"Nope. What's up?" I could hear road noise in the background and imagined Noah driving around downtown in the Bronco, waiting for a ride request to come in.

I didn't think about why I wanted comfort or to have someone cheer me up. Or why Noah's number was the one I'd dialed. I just let myself ask, "You want to meet me at Dottie's?"

His turn signal sounded through the tiny speaker, and I fought the urge to tear up as he changed direction before he even answered.

"Okay, but I get to pick the flavors."

"Deal," I replied quickly, voice a little choked.

A beat passed before Noah said softly, "You okay, Lu?"

"Yep!" My tone was overly bright, and I knew he heard it. "I'm five minutes away. I'll see you soon."

"I'll be there."

Our call disconnected, and I got myself under control. I didn't even know why I was emotional all of a sudden. But the urge to cry again rose swift and unwelcome the minute I walked into Dottie's five minutes later.

Noah stood by the counter, hands in the pockets of his jeans and a navy-blue hoodie covering his upper half. He smiled as I walked straight into him, my arms closing around his waist, clutching him tight as I fought the burning behind my eyes and the lump growing in my throat.

CHAPTER 12

Noah

Slowly, I brought my arms around Lu, who clung to me like a lifeline.

I felt my brows furrow in confusion. I'd never seen her like this. Lu was typically positive and upbeat—bright and bold and larger than life. She smiled all the time and made people feel welcome with a kind word wherever she went. Sunshine in human form.

But she felt small and vulnerable just now.

I banded one arm around her shoulders, enveloping and holding her close. With the other hand, I stroked gently up and down her back, moving with the intent to soothe over the fabric of her dark peacoat.

I'd heard something in her voice over the phone. I knew the

birthday dinner for her dad was tonight and, judging by the time, assumed she'd called me on her return trip down the mountain. Something had clearly happened, and she'd sought me out for comfort. I wasn't about to make her regret it. Everything about our relationship was new, but I was glad I was the one she'd reached for when she'd needed someone to hold on to.

I pressed a kiss to her temple and let my lips linger there before saying, "Everything okay?"

She nodded against my shoulder, and my concern ratcheted up a notch.

Several people came and went while we stood frozen in place, but I'd stay right here for as long as Lu wanted.

After another couple walked by with their cones and back out the door with a jingle of the front bell, Lu finally lifted her head and loosened her death grip on me.

"Thanks for meeting me," she said. Her gray eyes were dry, but she still didn't look or sound like herself.

"Slow night," I said, and she nodded. Then I answered with the truth. "But I wanted to see you, so I'm glad you called."

Her close-lipped smile had me reaching for her hand and tugging her up to the counter. I wanted to make her feel better—give her what she needed. Prove that calling me hadn't been a mistake. If she wanted to talk about whatever put that look on her face, then we would. But I wasn't going to push.

When the high schooler with the ice cream scoop came over, I ordered butter pecan for Lu—her mother's favorite, she'd told me a while back—and mint chocolate Oreo for me. I handed Lu both cups and paid despite her protests and led her back out to the Bronco.

"I'll drive you back. We can get the Jeep tomorrow," I said, opening the passenger door for her. "Hop in." She shouldn't be alone right now with whatever was bothering her, so the thought of driving separately didn't sit right.

She climbed into the car, still holding both cups in her grip. Before closing the door, I leaned in and pulled the seat belt carefully over one shoulder and buckled it in for her. She watched me with soft eyes, and while I was so close, I leaned in and pressed a kiss to her lips.

She tasted sweet, and I forced myself to pull away.

Once I got settled behind the wheel and started back out onto Main Street, I accepted my ice cream and drove in the direction of Lu's apartment complex.

We ate in silence for a few minutes before I tentatively asked, "So how was your dad's birthday thing?"

She ate a spoonful of dessert before replying. "It was fine. The stuffed mushrooms were good." My eyes drifted her way briefly while we waited at the stoplight. She sighed. "It was the same as usual. My stepmom and my stepsister mostly ignored me. Dad asked me a few questions about what was going on in my life. And then it was time to go home."

The part of me that felt protective of Lu wanted to ask why her dad never stood up for her. Why didn't he make more of an effort to integrate the two sides of his family? He couldn't really be so blind to how his wife and stepdaughter treated Lu, could he? But

I kept my mouth shut.

This dinner seemed to be par for the course, yet it clearly upset her. So I would be the ear she needed when she was ready to talk.

Lu was looking out the window and ignoring her ice cream when she admitted, "Kimberly didn't even tell me about the details of the dinner. She ignored my texts. I invited myself and found out about the reservation by calling the restaurant. If it had been left up to my stepmother, I wouldn't have even been there tonight."

Ah shit. "I'm sorry. That must have hurt."

I was the sort of person who would have said *fuck that.* Have your dinner, and if you don't want me there, so be it. But that wasn't Lu. I had a feeling she'd given her family unlimited chances, yet they still found new and inventive ways to let her down.

"It shouldn't hurt," she finally said just as I pulled into a parking space at Shady Peaks. "I should be used to it by now. And part of me is. But another, resentful part of me that usually stays pretty quiet feels exhausted by the prospect of doing this for the rest of my life."

"You shouldn't have to. You're his family too. You deserve to be in your dad's life without these ridiculous roadblocks in your way."

Lu spooned up another bite and held it there for a moment. "I don't even know what I'm doing wrong. Why she's never accepted me." She huffed. "I mean, my stepsister and I are never going to be friends. You can't be bullied by someone in high school and expect either one of us to think of the other as family."

I hated this girl I didn't know. Some immature mean girl who couldn't just grow the fuck up. And her petty-ass mother.

"None of this is your fault, Lu. You're obviously being the bigger person. Going out of your way and doing everything you can to fit into your dad's new life."

She glanced my direction and met my eyes for the first time since I'd started the car. "I know you think I'm stupid for trying, for—"

"I do not think you're stupid," I interrupted firmly. "I think you have a big, forgiving heart." And that her family didn't deserve her—her spineless dad included. There was no way he missed the animosity between Lu and her stepfamily. Either her father was willfully ignorant or he just didn't care. I didn't know which was worse in this scenario.

Either way, I hated seeing Lu so miserable over people who didn't fucking matter. Not that I could admit that. Especially not to someone who wanted the ideal—a sitcom family and the bonds of familial love.

I thought she should have higher expectations for the people she fought to keep in her life. But I didn't tell her that. I would have given up on all of those assholes a long time ago. But she wasn't me. And that was a good thing.

Lu was a good person, deep down. She was special. I'd known it from the first time I met her. But she didn't realize that love didn't have to be the people bound to you by blood. She could make her own family. Lu had Cody and her friend Emma, and this town that she loved. There were so many people everywhere we went who cared about her. And a very small voice that I refused to give too much weight to whispered that she had me too.

"But you wouldn't keep trying if they were *your* family," Lu said, pulling me out of my thoughts.

"Maybe not," I admitted. "But that doesn't make me right. That just makes us different."

She nodded and took another bite of ice cream. "Do you want to come in for a while? Until you get a ride request?"

"Do you want me to?"

"Yes," she replied without hesitation.

So we gathered our cups and Lu's gigantic purse and went inside her apartment.

I texted Jimmy on the way, letting him know I needed to take the rest of the night off. Lu was clearly upset about the evening's event. She'd sought me out for comfort, and I could do more than fit her between Huber rides. I'd keep her company, cheer her up, and be a sounding board for whatever she wanted to discuss. I'd stay with her in her apartment for as long as she needed me.

And I'd be lying if I said I hadn't thought about what had happened the last time I'd been here. But I liked being in Lu's space. It was comforting and warm, like her. Whenever we were together, Lu and I had fun. And spending the night had been really nice. The blow job hadn't hurt either. It was more than that, though. We were heading down a path. I could see it clear as day—a minefield of complications that simply came with getting to know someone. All the expectations and feelings that made a relationship a delicate balance. And my last one hadn't gone so well. Yet I wasn't eager to divert. I liked being with her. Lu was someone worth knowing, and honestly, trying to fight the pull I felt toward her was getting more difficult by the day.

I was a little surprised when we settled on Lu's couch, and she did something she hadn't done in a while. She opened her mouth and said, "I think the reason you moved here was to start over."

It wasn't a silly guess this time—not about beekeeping or cosmetology school or anything sure to make me laugh. I saw this for what it was . . . Lu asking me for the truth.

Meeting her knowing gray gaze, I forced my breathing to slow. The prideful parts of me would probably always feel a certain level of embarrassment associated with this summer. My beginnings in Cozy Creek were marred with the truth, as painful and humiliating as it had been. But somehow I knew that this girl wouldn't judge me for it.

Lu was kind and compassionate. She forgave her unworthy family members over and over again. Surely, she could forgive me for something that had happened before we'd ever even met.

I ran an uncomfortable hand along the scruff of my jaw. "In a way, yeah. I did come here to start over. I lost my job back in South Carolina. Something stupid that was all my fault. I was responsible for being on call, and I'd been distracted, so I'd let people down and cost the company a lot of money. I deserved to get fired."

"Everyone makes mistakes, Noah."

"Yeah, they do. And there are consequences for them."

"Did someone die?"

My brow furrowed. "No. I worked in IT."

"Then it was just a mistake."

I took in her fierce expression and the way she stood up for me without even knowing the full story, and I couldn't help but reach over and lace my fingers through hers. "It was. But it happened."

"How did that bring you here?" she asked.

"I'd been dating someone—online—who lived in Cozy Creek." Lu's eyebrows flew up. I guessed she hadn't been expecting that. And why would she? Lu didn't know how vigilant I'd been while driving around Cozy Creek, always on edge, in constant awareness.

But I went on. "When I lost my job and was spiraling, she said I should come here so we could be together."

I'd sold most of my stuff the week following my termination and made the trip out west to join Virginia in Cozy Creek. She'd promised to help me find an apartment and temporary employment. But when I got to Colorado, the woman I thought I'd been falling for was one who only existed in my mind. She'd played a game, and I'd been the loser. Her online persona had been just that—a facade, a character she'd been performing. The real Virginia was nothing like the woman I'd been dating for months, and she'd treated me like a pathetic stranger when I'd shown up on her doorstep.

"How long were you involved?" Lu asked gently.

"About six months. But we'd never met in person. A lot of calls and texts and video calls." I swallowed. This was the shit part. "So I packed up and drove out here. But when I got to town, she couldn't believe I actually came. I guess she liked messing with guys online and stringing them along. I don't know. But she acted like a different person when I knocked on her door. Seemed to think it was all a big joke."

"I can't believe you really came here. We don't even know each other. I thought we were just having fun and fooling around."

Those words would haunt me for the rest of my life. Not only because I'd trusted her, but mostly because I could no longer trust myself. I'd been conned by a woman who was so bored with her small-town life that she thought it would be fun to destroy mine. She probably had ten online boyfriends she was stringing along. I'd been the only one with the perfect setup and circumstances to see me down on my luck and desperate. And probably the only one dumb enough to fall for her shit.

Maybe if I'd stayed in South Carolina, she would have grown tired of me or just ghosted me one day when the fun wore off. But I'd never know.

"Oh my God, Noah." Lu pivoted on the couch to face me. She grabbed hold of my other hand attempting to draw my attention to her.

It had been easier to tell her the truth while staring at the blank television in front of us. I didn't need to see her face to know there was incredulous disbelief and a healthy dose of pity in there as well. I could feel how hot my cheeks had gone.

"Noah," Lu tried again, tugging our joined hands to her chest.

This time I did meet her gaze, allowing a small, sad smile.

"You have to know that none of that was your fault. I'm sorry, but this girl sounds like a sociopath. Only a monster would do something like that."

I nodded. "A monster I'd thought I'd been dating for six months."

Lu's face was intense. "She hid herself from you. You saw what she wanted you to see. I am so sorry that happened to you. God, after the job and the move. No wonder you didn't want to talk to me. You were stranded in this town. Somewhere you never asked to be."

Finally, she gave in to her instincts and lunged forward, hugging me hard. "This was not your fault. You didn't deserve any of it."

I wrapped my arms around her and nodded, not really knowing how to respond. I definitely blamed Virginia for what happened, but I also took a lot of the guilt on myself for trusting someone so blindly and for being so fucking wrong.

Lu sat back and eyed me with concern. "Did you . . . did you love her?"

My knee-jerk reaction was to say no, immediately and with little room for discussion. But I made myself sit there and really think about the answer in a way I hadn't allowed since staring around an empty hotel room in disbelief while I scrambled to pull a life together in Cozy Creek. I hadn't let myself think about Virginia when I was looking for an apartment or trying to find a job. Survival had been the only thing on my mind.

Finally, I glanced at Lu and shook my head. "She didn't break my heart, but she did crack me right down the middle. To before and after. Back when I trusted myself and then to now, questioning everything."

Lu nodded as if that made sense to her when I could barely even put it into words myself.

"I think I loved the idea of having someone," I admitted with some effort. "I've always been pretty monogamous. I liked being in a relationship. The comfort and support of having someone so tied to you. It had been a while before I met her—before I gave the online dating thing a try. So when we started to hit it off, I *wanted* to love her. You have to understand," I said, swallowing hard. "I was in my hometown just getting by, keeping my head down. I felt like I was on a dead-end road—a dead-end life. Then I met someone, and I felt excited about something for the first time in a very long while. But she was just a projection, only showing me what I wanted to see. She was an illusion."

"She was cruel," Lu said emphatically. "Playing games with you like that for her own amusement. And if I ever see her around town, I'll hit her with my Jeep."

My laughter burst out of me, so unexpected in this quiet apartment at a time when I felt my emotions vibrating on the surface of my skin and my shame on public display. But I was grateful. Lu always knew what to say and how to get me to breathe again.

She was still smiling while she held my hand—her thumb stroking gently over my knuckles. "We can take things slow—as slow as you want. Until you trust me. And more importantly, until you trust yourself again."

I was surprised when relief didn't accompany her statement.

I thought that was what I wanted—what I needed. Time and distance and irrefutable proof that my instincts weren't all wrong. But instead, I whispered, "I do trust you, Lu."

And it was the truth. This girl with her red lips and wild hair, who was friendly and kind and loved fiercely. I'd taken one look at her standing on the sidewalk two months ago and woken up. She was comfort and courage wrapped up in a package that stole my breath. Lu was the friend I was always meant to have, and I knew, deep down, that she would take care of my heart if I gave it to her.

Fighting my attraction to her proved futile. Ignoring her in a town the size of a postage stamp wasn't feasible. And besides all that, I didn't want to keep her at a distance any longer. I needed Lu in my life. She was inevitable. *We* were inevitable.

I didn't want to waste any more time waiting for my brain to catch up with my heart. Maybe my instincts weren't faulty like I'd thought. They'd brought me here, after all.

Leaning forward, I cupped her soft cheek. My other hand threaded into her blond waves as I brought my lips to hers. She tasted sweet like ice cream, and I licked into her mouth, slow and deep.

Her arms wrapped around my shoulders, and suddenly, I wanted to feel her everywhere—on top of me, beneath me, surrounding me, and squeezing every single inch.

Drawing her close, I helped her straddle my hips. She was warm as she settled against me, her shimmery copper skirt fanning out around us.

We made out with Lu on my lap, but it wasn't frantic and hurried like our actions had been in the past. There was gravity to what we were doing now as if we both knew this *meant* something. The first stop on the path to more.

Lu straightened, tugging on the hem of her shirt. I helped her bring the silky white fabric up and over her head. She wore a sheer bra of the palest pink, the edges lined with lace and a tiny bow in the middle. She looked so fucking pretty perched on top of me.

"Can I?" I said, my right hand molding to the warm flesh of her ribs.

"Yes, Noah," she whispered. "Yes to everything."

My hand snaked around to the center of her back, bringing her breasts forward. I covered one hard nipple with my lips and licked wetly against the delicate fabric. Lu squirmed, a choked sound leaving her throat as she threaded her fingers through my hair and held me to her.

Switching sides, I mouthed and tongued the pink tip, feeling her shift on top of me, trying to get closer. My dick strained behind the zipper of my jeans as Lu's hot center ground against me, seeking friction.

The temptation was there to get lost in the feel of her, this urgency between us giving way to rushed movements and instant gratification. I forced myself to focus. With my hands beneath her ass, I stood. Lu's legs locked around me as she squeaked in alarm. I gave her a little squeeze and a quick kiss as I walked us both toward her bedroom. The lamp atop her bedside table was already on, and I was glad. I wanted to look at her. I wanted to see us together this way.

After setting her down gently, I started removing the mountain of throw pillows on top of her bed. She laughed and climbed on, tossing a few of her own at me and on the floor. Smiling, I tugged my shirt off and joined her a moment later, urging her flat on her back. I kissed my way down her body, tasting her collarbone, her shoulder, the place in the center of her chest that pounded out a beat just for me.

When I got to the edge of her skirt, I looked up. "Good?"

"Wait," Lu answered breathlessly. I froze my movements, but she continued. "What about work? I don't want to distract you when you're on shift."

I smiled at her—always so kind and thoughtful. Even in this situation, half undressed and impatient for each other, Lu was thinking of me. "I texted Jimmy and told him I was taking the rest of the night off. Everything is fine."

Relief relaxed her features before a naughty grin tilted the corners of her lips. "So you're mine tonight?"

"I'm yours," I replied simply.

Resuming my attentions, I ran my hands up her thighs and hooked my fingers in the waistband of her underwear—pale and pretty, just like her bra—to tug them down, leaving the fabric of her skirt bunched above her thighs.

Lu let her legs fall wide as I settled between them. I parted her and gave a long, slow lick with the flat of my tongue. She was hot and wet and tasted amazing. When I peeked up, Lu had her head thrown back and an arm over her face. I smiled and went back to work. I kissed and sucked, licking her pussy top to bottom and side to side. She was twisting and restless after long minutes, so I slid a finger inside her and focused my attention back on her clit.

Slim fingers threaded into my hair and tugged as Lu moved against me, hips rolling to the beat of her pleasure. I added another finger and resisted the urge to grind against her bed. She was tight and wet and would feel so fucking good when I slid inside her. Pressure was building in me as Lu made these little sounds, growing more fraught and intense by the second.

"Right there," she moaned. "Right. There."

I kept doing what I was doing, not moving away an inch, tongue flicking her clit and fingers fucking into her.

Finally, her breathing hitched, and her body went rigid. Rhythmic pulses squeezed my fingers, and I gentled the strokes of my tongue as she came against my mouth. Her fingers still clutched my hair, and I didn't think she realized how hard she clung to me.

Smiling, I pressed kisses to her core, liking the way her breath caught each time I did.

"Come up here," she croaked.

I rested my head on her thigh and gazed up the length of her body. "You have to let go of me first."

Lu's fingers flexed in my hair. "Oh. Sorry." A little laugh sounded, and I felt it. "Did I hurt you?"

"Not even a little." I grinned.

She released me, and I climbed up to her, nosing at her pale skin as I went. Her cheeks were flushed, and those gray eyes heated as she took me in.

Lu had a condom waiting, and I had no idea where that had come from. "Good?" she repeated my question from earlier, and I could only nod.

Together, we wrestled off my jeans and boxer briefs. She shimmied out of her skirt, and I unclasped her bra. I hugged her close for a moment, just feeling her skin and her warmth. I thought I might never want to leave this bed, but then she pressed her hips up into mine, and I couldn't think anymore because my dick settled right where I wanted to be.

I made quick work of the condom and then kissed her slow and deep, pressing forward and into her at the same time, inch by agonizing inch.

My thoughts fractured, segmenting into the here and now. She was all snug heat and smooth skin. Wild blond hair all around us and arms holding me close. And then I heard her sigh right by my ear as I bottomed out inside her.

Pulling back, I asked, "Okay?"

It was her turn to nod. "You feel so good."

I felt a laugh bubble up in my throat. "No, Lu. *Christ.* You feel amazing."

And then she was grinning, and I was moving, ratcheting up the pleasure between us. Getting us closer and higher and within reaching distance together.

I buried my face in her neck. The warm vanilla scent of her skin washed over me as I rolled my hips. She made a sound that

I took as encouragement and prayed I wouldn't come right that second because she felt too good and too perfect, and I wanted her to be right here with me.

Lu tensed again, and then her orgasm moved through her in a rush, my name fast and light, repeating on her lips like a broken prayer.

I let myself go, moving with purpose despite knowing that this was probably going to kill me. Pleasure tightened all my muscles before gathering at the base of my spine. I thrust forward once, twice, and then lightning exploded behind my eyes.

Moaning into the soft skin of her throat, I felt Lu's nails scratch gently across my shoulder blades, and she held me tight—so tight. As if I would leave. As if there was anywhere else I could possibly want to go. She was sunlight, air, shelter—everything I'd ever wanted in my most desperate heart.

"It's not supposed to be like that," she murmured quietly, her lips grazing my temple as she spoke.

Raising my head to look at her, I asked, "What?"

"It's not supposed to feel that good—to feel that right."

I knew what she meant. First times were awkward with a lot of questions and uncertainty. It was hard to get lost in someone else when you were worried and overthinking every move you made. But she was right. This had been perfect. In fact, everything between us felt right—from the very beginning. We'd clicked on every level, and I wasn't surprised now that I'd just had the best sex of my life. It wasn't *just* sex. It was Lu.

So I brushed a strand of hair away from her damp forehead

and kissed the corner of her mouth. "But it's you and me, Lu. You knew it'd feel like this. We never stood a chance."

Her grin was wide and pleased, and she nodded, cupping my cheeks and kissing me again, over and over until she had her fill.

Finally, I got up and took care of the condom in the bathroom across the hall.

Padding back into the room, I noticed Lu's eyes moving over my still-naked body.

"You know, I'm feeling a little objectified," I teased.

She grinned, unrepentant. "You should be. But you can objectify me later."

I slid back under the covers, and Lu snuggled up against me, her soft skin a reminder of all the things we'd done tonight.

"Do you think Jimmy's mad that you took the rest of the night off?"

I brushed an errant blond curl out of my mouth and replied, "He seemed fine about it. Why?"

"You know I'm afraid of his New York mob connections."

I laughed. "You're a nut. He doesn't have mob connections." I frowned. At least I didn't think he did.

"You're staying the night, right?"

Leaving hadn't even crossed my mind. "If that's okay with you."

"More than okay," Lu said, her fingers drawing lazy designs across my torso. A moment of comfortable silence passed before she spoke again. "Thanks for riding to my rescue tonight."

Once again, my mind flashed back to the ice cream shop and

the way Lu had clung to me. I knew it had to be hard for her to admit how hurt she'd been by her family this evening.

I tightened my arms around her and hugged her close. "Anytime, Louie, Louie."

CHAPTER 13

Noah

"Hey, there's a poker game next week at the firehouse. You should come. You've met most of the guys."

We'd just hit the four-mile mark and were walking the last quarter of a mile toward the bakery as a cooldown when Cole Sutter, local fireman and my new running partner, spoke up. He hardly seemed winded in his navy Cozy Creek Fire Brigade tee shirt.

"Yeah, count me in." I'd never played poker before in my life, but I could watch some videos and probably figure it out.

He glanced at me sidelong, blue eyes amused and a barely restrained grin on his face. "Always looking for fresh blood."

"You mean fresh meat."

Cole finally laughed. "Come on. It'll be fun. You might even keep your money."

I snorted, doubtful. But it might be nice to have another extracurricular activity in Cozy Creek. I'd met the majority of the people on the fire brigade, and they all seemed nice. I usually met Cole there on his lunch break for our runs during the week. There were always other guys around and he'd been good about introducing me. We'd shoot the shit with the other guys while we stretched and warmed up.

Pace Leigh, one of the other firefighters with a ridiculous mustache, joined us for our runs when he was on shift, too.

We usually finished up at the bakery, where we snagged protein shakes, and I went upstairs to my apartment to shower afterward.

Crossing the street, we entered the Cozy Creek Confectionery, and the bell jingled over the front door. I took in the smell of fresh-baked bread and the line of people picking up something for lunch. Madison was working the counter. She was the granddaughter of the owner, and Cole had a huge thing for her. She was also my across-the-hall neighbor. We both lived above the shop, thanks to her grandmother, Gigi.

Madi caught our eyes and nodded toward the end of the counter. Two pale orange shakes waited in clear plastic cups.

Cole had no shame in walking right past the busy line of tourists and locals. I followed without making eye contact.

"Thanks, Madi," Cole said, before leaning his tall frame across the counter and smacking a kiss on the brunette's lips.

I pulled out some cash and dropped it on the counter while

Madison and Cole made googly eyes at each other. "Thanks, Madi," I echoed, without the kissing part.

She still looked a little dazed when she mumbled, "No problem, Noah."

"I'll see you tomorrow, Cole."

He turned to me. "Yeah. And don't forget poker next Wednesday. Learn to play between now and then."

I gave a little salute and made my way out to the back stairs and up to my apartment, sipping on my shake. I wondered if Lu knew how to play poker. Maybe she could teach me before next week. She was coming over in thirty. I could ask her then.

"Can you make it zoom in on the image if they hover the cursor over it?"

"Yep," I confirmed. "And I found a plug-in that will integrate with your online shop to correctly calculate shipping based on weight and geographic location."

"Oh, nice."

It was Thursday afternoon, and Lu sat beside me in a kitchen chair she'd dragged around to my side to see the screen better. We'd been working on her website for a couple of hours each day this week. She'd typically come over after my daily run with Cole, then we'd have lunch together and work on the specifics of her site. Then she'd usually hang out on my couch with her tablet, designing new art for her shop while I worked on websites for some of my other clients.

Becca, the graphic designer who'd been my first customer, had come through big-time in word-of-mouth recommendations. She had a steady stream of author friends reaching out to either build something new for them or consult on ways to improve what they already had. A lot of them were getting into direct sales for paperbacks, e-books, and audiobooks on their sites.

Lu had also introduced me to several local business owners interested in my services. The time was coming very soon when I'd need to quit driving for Huber and focus on my web design business full-time.

I was glad. I really was, but it felt weird to be putting down roots in Cozy Creek when I'd been planning my escape for so long. The idea of branching out and making more connections in town felt a little scary. Part of me was also concerned that I'd eventually run into Virginia. But it hadn't happened yet. It would be awkward for sure. But I was sure that with the way things had ended, she hadn't anticipated me hanging around.

It didn't matter. Despite my intentions, Cozy Creek was starting to feel like home.

Glancing at the curtain of blond hair to my right and the face drifting closer and closer to the screen, I realized the reason for that might be a person rather than a place.

"You know, you might need some readers, Luttle Old Lady."

She leaned back abruptly, and I fought a laugh.

"I do not. Your font is just really tiny." I raised my brows but said nothing. "Shut up! Okay, fine." Lu laughed. "Maybe a trip to the optometrist is in my future."

"You would look crazy cute with glasses," I offered.

"Really?"

"Yep. And you'd have the added benefit of actually being able to see, you nut."

"Fiiiiine," she groaned, and I leaned forward to kiss her. "Okay, I need to head back to my apartment. I have some orders to pack up for the week."

"Okay." I rose from my chair, a little stiff from how long we'd been working this afternoon.

Lu was sliding her ballet flats on—purple polka dot today—and grabbing her jean jacket out of the hall closet.

I liked having her in my space, I realized. She had a spot on the kitchen counter where she kept her keys and her water bottle. That giant purse of hers was taking up the armchair in the living room. There was a blue toothbrush in the bathroom and approximately eight thousand hair ties around the apartment courtesy of Lu Billings. And everything sort of smelled like vanilla for a while after she left. I did not hate it. And sort of looked forward to the day when it smelled like her all the time.

I watched her gather her things, knowing it was dangerous to rely on someone with anything as tenuous as feelings. But I couldn't seem to stop myself. Every time I saw Lu, I felt like I was losing bits and pieces of my heart to her, too cowardly to hand it over all in one go. At times, it was like ice cracking and breaking off into the ocean, while at others, it was an avalanche—out of control and unstoppable.

My thoughts were so loud, it was hard to believe she couldn't hear them from her place near the door. I snagged a hair tie off the kitchen table and walked toward her.

In the past week since I'd met her for ice cream, we'd spent every night together. Either I came to her place after driving for half the night or she fell asleep in my bed here, and I woke her up in really fun ways that she didn't seem to mind. We hadn't been dating for very long, but she was already so ingrained in my life that I knew I should be worried. But I just couldn't find it within myself.

This relationship—the healthy give and take, the affection, the mutual respect—felt so right, so true. It was wrong to compare past girlfriends, but I'd never felt for someone the way I felt for Lu. I'd known that what I'd had with Virginia hadn't been real. Nothing made that more glaringly obvious than experiencing it firsthand now.

I was happy. And it wasn't *just* because of Lu. I had work that fulfilled me and a routine, consistency. And I had friends in Cole and Pace and some of the other guys at the fire brigade. People waved and said hi when they saw me around town. It felt ... good.

Part of me wanted to raise the alarm and shout a warning, afraid that good things didn't come my way anymore. But I didn't want that fear to take over my life the way it had when I left South Carolina. I wanted to live a life where I wasn't constantly waiting for an asteroid to come down and blow it all apart.

"You coming over tonight?" Lu asked, tugging her hair out from beneath the collar of her jacket.

My shift driving for Jimmy started at five. I nodded and slipped the black elastic around her wrist in case she needed it. "I'll see you later."

She grinned and lifted on her toes to fit her lips to mine. "Bye, beekeeper."

I lowered my voice to something intent and whispered, "Bye, Luanne," against the shell of her ear.

She drew in a sharp breath, and I fought the urge to smile.

I'd have time later to make her shiver.

Just after two in the morning, I slid beneath the soft flannel sheets of Lu's bed. I'd finished up with my last fare twenty minutes ago—a few drunk locals needing a lift home from Bookers on Main Street. Using the spare key Lu had told me about three nights ago, I'd let myself in.

Now I was here, and she was warm beneath the covers in the dark of her bedroom. And she was—I paused, hands seeking her—definitely naked.

Grinning into the dark, I shucked my boxer briefs—my last remaining layer—and pressed myself to her back, spooning behind her. She was so warm and soft. I could feel my shoulders relax and tension leave my body as our skin made contact. Her hair was in a giant bun on the top of her head, so I put my lips against her nape and breathed in her sweet scent.

Lu arched against me when I sucked gently at the juncture of her neck and shoulder. She came awake slowly as I kept kissing her and brought my arm around her waist. Lu stretched like a cat, groaning and squirming in a way that had my erection further stiffening.

"Hey, you," she murmured, voice sleepy but pleased.

"It's Noah," I said before running my nose along the column of her throat up to her ear.

Despite the darkness, I could hear her smile in response to my teasing. I loved knowing that. Being so close, so familiar, that I could feel her reaction in my gut. "Thank you. I forgot who was on the schedule for tonight."

In reply, I scraped my teeth gently behind her ear.

She gasped and pushed herself back into me. My dick was nestled against her perfect ass, and I couldn't fight the urge to thrust and create some friction. I continued sucking and kissing her neck and shoulder as my hand drifted deliberately to the apex of her thighs. Lu parted for me, her hips rocking in time with my small movements.

"How was your night?" she asked a little breathlessly.

"Better now."

My fingers ghosted over her clit and down through her folds. She was wet and hot, slippery against my fingers.

Lu's breath hitched. "What time is it?"

"A little after two."

I sank a finger inside her. So fucking tight. The heel of my hand ground into her clit as she shifted. Her ass was stroking my dick with the rhythm of her hips, and I swallowed hard to keep from lifting her thigh over mine and pushing into her sweet pussy.

But then suddenly, she had a condom in her hand and passed it to me. I ripped the wrapper and slid it on as Lu canted her hips, angling her ass and arching her body before resting her thigh atop mine.

"Oh," she breathed as I lined myself up at her entrance and eased my way in, slow and deliberate.

Once I was fully seated and could go no further, I reached around with my hand, smoothing up the slight curve of her stomach, over her breasts, to rest at the base of her throat. Rolling my hips, I made my thrusts slow and deep. Relaxed in my arms, she was all snug heat, and I wasn't going to last.

I picked up my pace when her eager hand reached back to feel my flexing ass. Little nails dug into my skin, and my eyes rolled back. "Shit," I hissed.

Lowering my hand back down, I felt where we were joined, then brought two fingers to circle her clit. I needed to get her there before this was all over. She felt too fucking good, and the fact that she'd been waiting for me, naked in this bed, made me—

Lu moaned and stiffened before I felt her walls pulsing around me. That was all I needed. My thrusts grew wild as I chased my own orgasm, detonating with an intensity that had stars flashing behind my closed eyelids.

Minutes, hours, maybe days later, I managed to roll onto my back, breathing hard and staring at the dark ceiling of Lu's bedroom. The bed dipped as she shifted closer. Her shadow a midnight outline hovering above me. She peppered kisses all over my face, and I couldn't help the dopey-ass grin that came over me. God, she was cute.

And that had been so good. It kept being good. From the blow job to our first time together nearly a week ago to now, and every time in between, it was just getting better and better.

I could feel myself falling in deeper—wanting more with Lu until I didn't think it would ever be enough. That sunlamp feeling from the very beginning, warming me from the inside out was now the sun itself shining down over both of us.

Eventually, she left to clean up, and I did the same. We stayed naked and climbed back into bed together, Lu snuggled up against my chest while pieces of hair that escaped her bun tried to infiltrate my airways.

"How was your night?" I finally said. "I meant to ask earlier and got distracted."

Her lips curved, and I felt the movement against my chest. "It was good. I got all my orders packed up to take to the post office tomorrow on my way to the farmers' market."

"Good. I'll drop by and bring you a late lunch at your booth."

"That would be great. Thank you. You could go by Tres Chicas and talk to them about the website they want. I think they need a way to integrate their calendar into the site so people know where their food truck will be on any given day."

"I can do that," I said around a yawn. "It's Marta, right?"

"Yep, and her sisters Luce and Gracie. I went to high school with Luce."

"The six degrees of Cozy Creek."

Lu snorted. "Try three degrees max."

That was okay. I didn't mind the small-town aspect. It's what I was used to, after all.

"Did you always want to live in a small town?" I was curious about why Lu came back here after college. I knew she wanted to be close to her dad, but it was pretty clear that things with her stepfamily hadn't progressed the way she'd hoped.

"Sure. I'm not really built to be in a big city, surrounded by strangers who never wave or talk to one another. I like how friendly and neighborly Cozy Creek is. I like that I can meet new people during tourist season, but that I can run into every teacher I've ever had down at the General Store. Or that my favorite restaurants know I'm a regular and have my take-out order memorized. It's comfort and consistency and knowing that I have a place I belong. If I had to be a tiny gear in a big machine, I'd probably get lost."

"I don't think you could lose yourself anywhere, Lu. You stand out wherever you go. In the best way."

She was quiet for a moment before admitting, "I guess I'm holding out hope that I'll have a real family someday with my dad and my stepmother and stepsister. Sunday dinners and birthdays and holidays." Her voice went from wistful to unsteady from one statement to the next. "Part of me thinks that if I'm not here, in town, in their faces and calling to check in, that my dad will forget I exist entirely. He'll have Kimberly and his new daughter and *that* will be his family. And that will be enough."

I tightened my arms around her, trying to ease the hurt and

knowing there was no way I could. Comfort could only go so far. But sometimes it was enough to pull you back from the brink.

She swallowed against my chest, and I hated that she was trying to hold herself together. Always making the best out of whatever shitty situation she was in. "But Cozy Creek is where my mother was born and raised. She loved it here, and I have so many happy memories because of her."

"Does she still have family here?" I wondered gently.

"No. Mom lost her parents before I was born. No siblings or cousins or anything, but I wish I could have known that side of my family. She named me after her grandmother who was from a tiny town in North Carolina called Kirby Falls. Luanne Billings the original agreed to move here with her husband because of the mountains. She said that while they were bigger and sharper than the mountains back home, they would do in a pinch."

I smiled, lips still pressed against her hair. "I like that."

"Me too."

I thought she might have fallen off to sleep, but suddenly Lu said around a yawn of her own, "I was thinking. What if you built an app for Jimmy? For ride requests. Then people wouldn't have to call him every time, which is, frankly, archaic and offensive."

I laughed but then thought about what Lu was saying. It was a really good idea.

"Do you think Jimmy would go for that?" she asked, her voice getting low and sleepy.

I'd been keeping her up too much, but I couldn't make myself regret it if I got to have her like this—warm in my arms.

"He might. Especially if I did it first and then showed him after. It would be way more convenient, and he could be a little more hands off, have some freedom untethered to his phone. He's stubborn but efficient. This might be right up his alley." Maybe it could be a parting gift for when I had to put in my notice soon.

As if reading my mind, Lu mumbled, "Maybe then he won't kill you for quitting to go work for yourself."

I smiled and pressed a kiss to her forehead. "He's not going to kill me." I still wasn't one hundred percent on that.

Then we went quiet, Lu's chest rising and falling evenly against me.

I took a deep breath full of contentment and peace and felt another little piece of my heart chip away and attach itself to the woman by my side.

CHAPTER 14

Lu

In my mind, I had a highlight reel of memories from the Fall Festival from the time I was tiny—four or five years old—until my mom passed away when I was fifteen. I'd attended in recent years too, usually with Cody. And a couple of years ago Emma visited and went with us.

But the year I turned ten really stuck out in my mind.

I hadn't been invited to a sleepover birthday party for one of the girls in my class. I remembered feeling completely devastated that I'd been left out. But my mom had done her best to cheer me up. She'd even done a fancy fishtail braid on my long hair. When she and Dad took me to the Fall Festival on the same weekend, they'd ridden rides with me and played carnival games. They definitely spent more money than they should have to keep me entertained and pull me out of my rejection funk.

At some point during our visit to the farm, we'd run into all the girls from my class who'd been invited to the sleepover that night. They wore matching tee shirts and gathered around the entrance to the corn maze. Most of the girls said hi and a few of them even asked me to join them and go through the maze together.

A part of me had wanted to abandon my parents and have fun with my friends. Probably that part that was desperate to be included. But I knew not everyone—the birthday girl specifically—wanted me there. And when I'd turned back to see my mom with a worried frown on her face, I knew that I'd rather be with her and my dad anyway. They'd loved me enough to try to cheer me up and make something special out of the day.

I'd spent the remainder of the Fall Festival making s'mores at the bonfire with my parents, grateful I had two people who loved me so much.

Not to say I didn't have typical kid moments of being an unappreciative little shit. But on that day, I was happy. *We* were happy.

And I was so ridiculously excited to take Noah around at the Fall Festival and introduce him to one of my favorite Cozy Creek celebrations.

It was a gorgeous Saturday afternoon in October. The air was crisp and cool—perfect for the black-and-white houndstooth scarf I had wrapped around my neck.

I stood on the sidewalk next to my building, waiting. I could have stayed inside the apartment, but this was more fun. Reminiscent of our first encounter, I sipped an iced coffee. Except this time, I had a second drink in my hand as the baby-blue Bronco turned into the parking lot.

Noah stopped beside me, the window already rolled down. "What's up, Louisiana Hot Sauce?"

I grinned. "Ohhhh. I like that one. Wait, is that because I rocked your world last night?"

His lips twitched. "Yes. And because you spice up my life. Come on, we have a hot date. I have a tractor to drive."

My grin went nowhere as Noah hopped out, accepted his drink, and opened the passenger door for me.

I shoved my purse down by my feet before I gave him a sympathetic look and replied, "You know they don't actually let you drive the tractor. You ride in a long trailer connected to the back. They just scatter some hay on the seats and call it a hayride."

He'd been driving slowly through the half-empty parking lot when he stopped the vehicle abruptly at my words. "What? I was promised a tractor. That's it. We're not going."

I laughed as he put the SUV in reverse and looked over his shoulder to back up.

We made it a few feet before he stopped and put the Bronco in drive again, shooting me a smile. I thought back to that first Huber ride. When he was so cautious and careful with me, distrustful and fighting his amusement. Now, sprawled in the driver's seat with his gray flannel and dark jeans, Noah looked relaxed and . . . happy.

I'd been so determined to see him settled in Cozy Creek. I'd encouraged him to branch out into the community, introducing him to people and taking him to different restaurants. All along, I'd wanted to be the friend he needed—a person here who he could count on.

His hair was longer and his smiles genuine, the tense line of his shoulders giving way to relief. He looked more at ease than I'd ever seen him. More Noah—the real Noah. And the very scary truth was that I was happy too. So happy spending our time together. Living this life with him. It was new, sure, but this thing between us felt right. Like Noah Cooper was meant to be a part of my life. A huge part.

I knew he'd think that was silly. That I was being fanciful or that fate didn't work like that, especially with how he'd ended up in Cozy Creek in the first place. But, deep down, I knew that Noah was mine, and I was his. And this was all just the beginning.

"Why are you staring at me like that? Did you poison my coffee?"

Resisting the urge to laugh, I deadpanned, "Just calculating how much I can get for your organs."

His laughter shot out of him, easy and free. Amusement lingered in his hazel eyes for a long time.

I loved when I caught him off guard like that. Those moments of freedom were growing more and more frequent. I sincerely hoped he always felt safe with me, like he was able to lower that drawbridge so I could get across the moat protecting his heart.

"Here," he said, passing me his phone. "Pick some music."

Grinning, I took the phone from him. My thumb must have bumped the notes app while we made the transfer because a little yellow digital sticky note popped up on the screen.

I shouldn't have looked. It was an invasion of privacy. But my brain was slowly registering what made up the list, and I couldn't have looked away if the phone caught fire.

Lucille Ball

Luella De Vil

Louie Anderson

Lou Bega

Louie Armstrong

Lu-ke Skywalker

...

My eyes went wide, and I glanced at Noah. His gaze was focused on the road, so I quickly turned my attention back to his phone. I closed the notes app and opened his music to find a playlist he'd made.

"Why are you smiling like that? Did you pick a boy band to torture me with?"

I startled in my seat, but my ridiculous grin stayed put. He was too sweet. Too precious for this world. He had a list of nicknames on his phone. Nicknames for me.

My heart might actually burst.

"No boy bands," I promised. "Just happy."

"Me too, Lewey Decimal System." His hazel eyes lingered on my face for a moment before sliding back to the highway. But he was still smiling too.

The remainder of the ride to the farm was comfortable as we sipped our drinks and listened to Noah's playlist.

We parked in a field with locals and tourists alike. A big archway at the entrance to the farm was flanked on either side by hay bales, corn stalks, sunflowers, and pumpkins in all shapes and sizes. Halloween was at the end of the month. Maybe Noah would want to pick some up from the pumpkin patch on our way out and carve them together. Main Street always hosted trick-or-treating, and I set up my DeLuLu Designs booth in the town square and handed out candy with the other local businesses and shop owners. And maybe we could do that together too.

Forcing myself to holster those rampant thoughts, I smiled as I took in the Fall Festival in all its glory. I loved it here, even with so many people milling about. It made me think of coming here as a kid, high on excitement and swinging on the arms of my parents. We'd ridden the rides and eaten junk food and had the best time. This autumn event was intrinsically tied to memories of my mom. There was no way I'd ever skip it. And I was pretty excited to share this part of Cozy Creek and myself with Noah.

He handed over our tickets to the teenager in the entrance booth and reached for my hand. "Okay, expert. Where to first? Teach me your ways."

I grinned and led him toward the row of carnival games.

An hour later, I wore a hat made of colorful balloons twisted together by the local balloon artist as I scanned the entrance to the farm. Noah had a stuffed sloth that I'd won in the ring toss game around his neck with the Velcro hands firmly latched in front of his throat. I'd named it Paloma and told him to treasure it always.

"Cody just texted," I told him. "Are you sure you don't mind if he hangs out for a bit? He has work this evening, so he can't stay long."

"Why would I mind?" Noah frowned. "He's your best friend, and so far, our only interaction was him bossing me around. It's like he's my best friend already too."

My laughter choked off as I spotted Cody coming our way. "Oh my God."

Noah stood next to me. "Is he wearing...?"

"Yeah," I managed while wheezing.

"Hey, y'all!" Cody cried out when he reached us. "Why are you breathing like that?" He turned to Noah as I bent over. "What did you do to her?"

"Nothing, man," Noah managed. "Good to see you."

I finally straightened and wiped my eyes. "Why are you dressed like that?"

My friend stood tall in black cowboy boots, tight dark-wash denim, a pale green shirt with pearl snap buttons, and perched on the top of his head, a straw cowboy hat.

Cody made a face. "I'm festive."

"Cowboys are not fall-specific," I argued. "They exist year-round."

"Maybe I wanted to nab myself a rancher from Montana!"

Noah cleared his throat. "Well, those would be the jeans to do it in."

"Thank. You," Cody replied pointedly as if that had been a compliment.

I reached forward and hugged my friend. "God, I love you. You're amazing."

Cody sniffed. "I know it." But his arms closed around me, and I breathed in his familiar cologne.

Pulling back, I asked him, "What do you want to do? I know you don't have long before you need to go to work."

I really wanted Noah and Cody to get along today. They both meant so much to me, and they'd gotten off to a weird start when Cody had forced us to talk and get our shit together. These two were the most important people in my life, so today's gathering was a big deal.

"Did you do the corn maze or the hayride yet?"

"Nope," Noah answered. "We rode some rides and played some games. Lu inhaled a funnel cake. That's about it."

I whacked Noah in the stomach. "I offered you some of that funnel cake."

Cody snorted. "Yeah, right. He would have lost a finger."

And then my boyfriend and my best friend cracked up and high-fived, and I wasn't even a little mad about it.

We spent the next thirty minutes bickering our way through the corn maze. I used my phone to find the map on the farm's website and left them to it for some bonding. Using the extra time once I'd reached the exit, I went over and grabbed some cotton candy from a nearby cart. I was waiting on a bench when they emerged—high-fiving again like ridiculous bros—and spotted me with my snack.

"Time for the hayride, LuLu," Cody called out as they approached.

Noah leaned over and snatched a bite of cotton candy out of my hand before kissing me on the lips. He tasted sugar-sweet and something about the public display of affection had me smiling like a goof. And when he grinned back just as widely, my stomach gave a helpful flip. I ignored the gagging face Cody was making in the background.

We walked toward the rear of the property, where a group gathered to wait for the next hayride behind a thin rope barrier. Noah spotted a few members of the fire brigade among the crowd and said hello. It felt really good to see him becoming part of the community.

"I still think I should be allowed to drive the tractor," Noah said while we watched the farm vehicle approach with a large trailer and all its passengers.

Cody replied seriously, "You know, I bet they'd let you drive the tractor if you looked the part. You can borrow my hat."

The tractor pulled to a stop, and the current festival-goers disembarked out the back of the trailer.

Noah hummed like he was considering Cody's offer. "Pretty sure cowboys drive horses, but nice try."

I cackled while Cody rolled his eyes good-naturedly.

And then it was our turn. We climbed up and settled on the hay-strewn seats, taking in the bright afternoon sun and the beautiful landscape. I breathed in the fresh air as Noah threaded our fingers together, that ridiculous stuffed sloth still wrapped around his neck.

I was so happy to be sharing this with him—something that I loved in my town. A place that held such wonderful memories. It would never be the same as visiting the Fall Festival with my mom and dad. That was a bittersweet part of my past. And maybe things with Dad and Kimberly and Ginny were never going to be what I had hoped, but this right here, with Noah, felt special in an entirely different way.

I squeezed his hand and tugged it into my lap. I could make new memories in Cozy Creek. Trying to recreate something made it that much harder to snap into place. I couldn't force my dad and stepfamily to fit into the same space—the same expectations—I had for what a family should look like. I was just setting myself up to fall short.

But this, here and now with Noah, didn't feel like I was missing out on anything at all.

"Okay, so are you going to raise or call?"

Noah eyed the stack of Sour Patch Kids in front of him. "I don't know how I'm supposed to want to win when the pot is this awful candy."

"It's all I had in the house, and apparently, you need to learn how to play poker by Wednesday."

Noah's night off was tomorrow, and he'd mentioned watching

some online videos to prepare for his hangout at the firehouse. I was trying to be chill about his date with the fire brigade, but I was, honestly, so excited that Noah was making friends. I wanted so much for Cozy Creek to feel like home to him. We'd had a great time at the Fall Festival this past weekend. He and Cody had gotten along and seemed to have a great time.

I knew that the more settled Noah felt here, the more likely he'd want to stay. He'd never come out and said he was planning on leaving Colorado. I didn't think anything really drew him back to South Carolina. Yet now knowing how Noah had ended up in Cozy Creek, I wouldn't blame him if he'd wanted to take off at the first opportunity. It was so hard to believe that anyone could be cruel enough to do what his ex had done. Playing games with Noah's life was just as bad as playing games with his heart.

Petty though it may be, I was curious about the mystery ex-girlfriend. Cozy Creek wasn't a big town by any stretch of the imagination. Sure, there were residents I didn't know. But it didn't stop me from wondering who had taken such joy in kicking Noah when he'd been down. I didn't want to come right out and ask. If Noah wanted me to know, he'd tell me, I supposed. And if we ever ran into the sorry excuse for a human being, I'd give her a piece of my mind.

A big part of me worried Noah wouldn't want to stay once he'd gotten his feet back under him. I didn't want him to leave. I was falling for him. It was as simple as that. And if he decided to go, I didn't know what I'd do. But manipulating him to stay wasn't an option.

I just had to hope that despite how things had started for Noah in Cozy Creek, the desire to stay would be stronger than any bitterness toward his ex. Maybe if he had a job he enjoyed, friends he could count on, and . . . me—maybe that would all be enough.

"Raise or call, beekeeper?" I repeated. Noah was the dealer this round and I'd already raised during the first round of betting.

He shot me a look from his slouched position across my kitchen counter. "Call," he replied, tossing the appropriate number of red and orange candies into the central pile.

He then burned a card off to the side before placing down the turn card.

I peeked at my hand and then looked back at Noah, who was concentrating hard, his hazel eyes narrowed at the cards he held.

Resisting the urge to smile, I placed my hand facedown on the granite countertop. "Maybe you just need some more motivation." Then I reached down for the hem of my sweater and dragged it over my head. "I raise you one shirt."

Noah sat up straighter, a smirk on his lips. "I'll call." In a move that all hot guys seemed to be masters of, he reached back over his shoulder with one hand and pulled his black tee shirt up and over, baring his lean torso.

Play continued until I was down to only socks and underwear, and it was time to show our hands.

Noah revealed a low-ranking pair and grinned. "I've got nothing." But he didn't seem mad about it. Not even when I revealed my full house.

I laughed. "Then why did you keep betting?"

"You kept pulling clothes off. I wasn't about to fold and make you stop."

Shaking my head in amusement, I stood and gathered up the cards. "You'll probably want to keep your pants on over at the firehouse."

"That won't be a problem," he replied, rising and moving around the counter toward me. "But I will have to try not to think about these lessons. Getting hard at a table full of firemen might be awkward."

My laughter drifted off on a sigh as Noah brushed my hair to the side and kissed my neck, his lips so soft and warm. Standing behind me, I could feel how hard he was. The thin fabric of his boxer briefs did little to hide the way he wanted me. I arched against him, desperate to get closer—to always be this close.

Noah's hands came around my body, and I leaned back into him, so warm and eager. His fingers skimmed my skin in a way that had me shivering.

I abandoned the cards and turned in his arms, feeling that same sense of rightness—the magical way we seemed to click. Like two magnets snapping together, unable to resist how good and true it felt when we were in the same orbit.

He lifted me onto the counter and stepped between my spread thighs, and then I stopped worrying about poker lessons or staying in Cozy Creek because Noah was here—right here, lighting me up and holding me tight.

I didn't want him to ever let go.

CHAPTER 15

Time floated by like a dream, and I floated with it. Weeks had passed with Noah. We'd made memories in Cozy Creek this autumn: the Fall Festival at Sutton Farms, trick-or-treating in the town square, costume contests, and pet parades downtown with the locals. We were all in with Cozy Creek and with each other.

It was early November, and the weather was changing, but things with Noah were steady. I loved our routine and all the time we were able to carve out for ourselves. The late nights in bed and sharing the same space. We grabbed drinks with Cody when he was free, and Noah joined me on Fridays at the farmers' market throughout the last month.

The part I loved about having a new relationship was how it seamlessly eased its way into comfort and domesticity. We were still getting to know each other, but there was depth and contentment. It wasn't settling but rather settling in.

Our lives were stitching themselves together. He was my best friend, and I was his. This was everything I'd ever wanted in a relationship. Someone to hold my hand as well as my heart.

Everything was great. So I wasn't sure why I was so nervous about bringing Noah to meet my family.

I'd texted my dad to check in earlier in the week, and he mentioned Ginny's upcoming return to work at the ski resort. We'd chatted for a bit back and forth, and he'd invited Noah and me over for dinner this weekend. Dad had seemed interested in meeting my boyfriend, but something about sharing the spotlight with Ginny made me feel uneasy. I'd never brought a guy home before. My last real relationship had been years ago in college, and he'd never made it back to Cozy Creek to meet my dad before we'd broken up.

Part of me worried that Ginny would make things uncomfortable or try to make me look bad in front of Noah. I hadn't confessed our turbulent history or the extent of Ginny's animosity toward me. The shameful part of me that couldn't make my stepsister like me was embarrassed. Not to mention the fact that I knew how Noah felt about maintaining unhealthy relationships.

But I was slightly reassured by the fact that she generally behaved herself in front of Kimberly and my dad.

Still, my hands fidgeted restlessly on the steering wheel of the Jeep as I drove us across town to Dad and Kimberly's house.

"Hey, so I gave Jimmy my notice."

I turned in surprise at Noah's declaration. I knew that business had picked up with his website, but I hadn't known he was this close to going it on his own. "Oh my gosh! That's amazing. I'm so happy for you."

"Thanks." Noah's grin was pleased, if a little embarrassed. He was going to need to get used to receiving compliments. He'd really put himself out there with his own business, and I was so proud of all his hard work.

I couldn't imagine showing up in a small town with nothing—no support, no friends, no place to live. But Noah hadn't shut down or backtracked. He'd moved forward and taken control.

"How did Jimmy take it?" I asked, focusing back on the road when all I really wanted to do was bail on dinner and go get celebratory tacos and margaritas.

Noah turned a little in his seat to face me. I noticed the scruff on his jaw was gone. He was clean-shaven for the first time since I'd met him. He'd taken care with the longer dark strands on the top of his head. Maybe I wasn't the only one nervous about tonight.

"He was mostly okay about it," Noah replied. "I showed him the app I built."

"The guilt app," I clarified. "The please-don't-murder-me app."

Noah laughed. "Yeah, that. He clicked around a lot before narrowing his eyes at me and saying he'd think about it while he looked for my replacement. I'm pretty sure he's going to go for it. He's called me twice since to ask questions about it. I'm fairly

209

confident he won't put a horse head in my bed."

I snorted at that.

Peeking in the rearview mirror, I braked at the stop sign in my dad's neighborhood. Then I leaned over and pulled Noah in for a big hug. "I'm really proud of you. It's going to be great. You don't have to worry."

I felt his arms squeeze me as he let out a breath, one I thought he'd been holding for a long, long time.

I had some experience starting my own business. It involved a lot of second-guessing and fear. Impostor syndrome was real. But at some point, you had to let the results speak for themselves. If you worked hard and put in the effort to make something a success, then you had to own it when success actually came calling.

Noah had clients. Noah had so many clients, he had a waiting list of people who wanted to work with him. There would always be a little bit of fear and a voice asking if those opportunities would dry up on down the road. But that's where the work came in. And I believed that Noah could do this. Quitting Huber had been like cutting the cord on a safety net. That job had been guaranteed income and the backup parachute in his Colorado free fall. But Noah was in a good place. He could focus his energy on making Ungoliant Web Design his priority.

The site he'd built for me was amazing. Direct sales had already made an impact on my bottom line.

"Thanks, Beluga."

I smiled against the fabric of his dark jacket, wondering if he'd ever run out of Lu nicknames for me, unbearably grateful for his sweet teasing.

We spent the remainder of the drive talking about Noah's current clients and some of the cool things he was working on. I tried not to let my nerves get the best of me and really focus on what Noah was saying.

But when I pulled into the driveway and shifted the Jeep into park, Noah pried my hands off the steering wheel. "What's going on, Lu? Why are you so nervous?"

I shook my head, unable to meet his gaze. "I don't know."

"Are you . . . worried they won't like me?"

I pivoted so quickly, I thought my neck might crack. "No! God, No. That's not it at all. I'm just— It's not—" I stopped and took a deep breath and tried again. "I know how they are. And I'm just scared for you to see it."

Noah frowned, his dark eyebrows drawing together. "What do you mean?"

Sighing, I let the admission come. "I just wish things were different. We're going to go in there, and it's going to be awkward. It's never not been awkward, ever, in ten years. My dad . . . he means well. And he loves me. He just doesn't really know me anymore. And he doesn't put in a whole lot of effort. And my stepfamily will ignore you at best or try to embarrass me in front of you at worst. I don't know. I just know how you feel about me wasting my time on them and—"

"Lu, hey." He quickly interrupted my frantic rambling. He reached for my hand and held it, drawing my attention. "I'm not judging you, or whatever you're thinking. There is nothing wrong with wishing for the family life you've always wanted. You are so positive and optimistic. If anyone could make it happen, it's you. We will go in there together and do this. Teammates, okay? It might be awkward and uncomfortable, but I won't judge you for their behavior. I'm here for you. Not them."

I nodded. Closing my eyes, I forced myself to take another deep breath.

A hand cupped my cheek and guided me closer. Noah's lips slotted themselves between mine, and he kissed me tenderly. It was a kiss of partnership. One filled with reassurance for all the words he'd just said. I returned his promise and affection, knowing that everything would be okay.

When Noah finally pulled away, he made sure to meet my eyes. His hand smoothed back the hair at my temples, and he nodded. "Good?"

"Good," I promised, feeling the truth of it settle all the restless energy I'd been fighting on the drive over.

We got out of the Jeep, and I led Noah in through the open garage door. Dad had music on, like always. It was the Joni Mitchell record I'd given him for his birthday. That knowledge helped to calm me even more.

But Dad wasn't in the kitchen when we entered. Neither was Kimberly. My stepsister, Ginny, sat on one of the barstools at the center island, looking at something on her phone. She didn't even glance up as I said hello and tension coiled. It was going to be how it always was with her.

But then my attention was diverted because I felt Noah stop moving abruptly. His hand pulled out of mine.

I glanced back over my shoulder in confusion to see him frozen on the threshold, staring forward, face stricken like he'd seen a ghost.

And that was when I heard Ginny say, "Is this, like, some kind of joke?"

Looking back and forth between a stunned Noah and an incredulous Ginny, I felt my stomach drop. Realization hadn't claimed me, but it was starting to creep in at the edges. My body got the message first and dread pooled in my belly. Something was very wrong.

Noah ran a hand across his smooth jaw as Ginny looked at me with delight. "You really brought my sloppy seconds to dinner, Luanne? Holy shit."

Kimberly and my dad chose that moment to enter the kitchen amid this tense standoff.

I didn't know what to say. I didn't know what to do. I could hardly breathe through my dawning comprehension.

Ginny. It was her. My stepsister was the reason Noah was in Cozy Creek. She had been the girl who'd catfished him and messed with his head. The person he thought cared about him. The reason he'd shut down his instincts and punished himself and pushed me away.

I felt sick.

Turning my back on my family, I begged, "Noah."

But he was already taking a step back in retreat, his head shaking in disbelief.

"Lu, what's the matter?" My dad's voice was concerned, but I couldn't deal with that right now.

In the next blink, Noah was out the door and gone.

🍃 *Noah* 🍃

Blood rushing in my ears, I took off down the driveway, bypassing the Jeep and going straight for the road.

"Noah, please!" Lu called from behind me, but I couldn't turn back.

Mortification churned in my gut. What were the fucking odds?

When I'd seen Virginia sitting in that kitchen, completely unexpected and out of context, everything had just sort of ground to a halt. My body stopped moving forward as if I'd hit a force field. Warnings blared in the back of my mind as I fought to make sense of my ex-girlfriend's presence in that house.

I had a vague recollection of Lu calling her stepsister Ginny. But the Virginia I'd known had never once mentioned a nickname or any family beyond her mom and dad. I thought she was an only child.

Part of me considered that this whole dinner might have been arranged as some sort of sick joke, but one look at Lu and I could see her putting the pieces together. The realization was stark on her pale face. No cunning or deception there. She was as blindsided as I was.

Quick shuffling footsteps reached me a moment before Lu snagged my arm and moved to block my path. "Noah, wait. I didn't know. I didn't know."

I stopped walking, but I couldn't look at her. Shame and humiliation over this fucked-up situation kept me from meeting her gaze. At the knowing I'd see there. The pity, the understanding. She'd be sorry for something that wasn't even her fault. Uncomfortable once again among her family for an entirely different reason.

"I can't talk about this right now, Lu." My voice was dead, utterly devoid of emotion. I needed to shut it all down so I could get out of here and process this on my own—figure out where to go from here.

"Okay," she agreed. "Let's go. I'll take us home."

Us.

Jesus.

Discomfort had me pulling away from her touch. Didn't she see how unbelievably messed up this was? Her stepsister was my ex-girlfriend. Her stepsister was the girl who'd tricked me and lied to me for months, for sport. She was the whole damn reason I was in this town in the first place. Virginia—Ginny—was the family that Lu was so desperate to win over.

I ran a shaking hand down my face. "I need to be alone right now."

"No," Lu begged. "Just let me take you away from here."

But I needed to be away from her, too. Couldn't she see that?

A new layer of pain and regret had just wrapped itself around my life in Cozy Creek. My presence here was a literal disaster. Lu wasn't getting it. How did we come back from something as twisted and wrong as this? I really didn't know. I needed time.

I shook my head, but Lu ignored me, reaching for my hand again. "Noah, I had no idea that Ginny was your ex."

I nodded. It was all I could manage. The words were white noise vibrating against my skull as I grew more and more agitated and overwhelmed.

"You never told me her name," she continued. "I didn't know, I swear. I never would have set you up that way."

I knew she hadn't. But I couldn't get the words out. A phantom hand gripped my throat. It wouldn't allow the words to escape, and I could hardly breathe around them.

I started walking again, but Lu clung to me and kept right on going. "I'm so sorry for what she did. I'll never forgive her. I'll—"

"Lu!" I exploded. The swirling mass of anger and disbelief ricocheting around inside me had found an outlet. She wasn't a fair target, and I knew it. But desperation and proximity put the bullseye on her back just the same. "Just stop. I need some time. I can't think."

"But I want to help."

"I don't want you to," I snapped in irritation. Then I jerked free of her grip. "I need you to stop. Stop pushing and pushing. Just back off right now and let me go. Forcing this isn't going to make it any better."

She absorbed the words like a blow, her face stricken in the orange glow of the streetlight.

I had a moment to regret what I'd said but self-preservation won out before I could make myself fix what I'd broken.

I stepped back as her head dropped to stare at the ground beneath her ballet flats.

I opened my mouth to say . . . something. But when the words wouldn't come—when I couldn't make myself be the person she needed—I moved around her instead.

And then I walked away.

Anger at myself and Virginia and this whole ruined night fueled my steps. I needed to get away from the humiliation burning a path through me. The farther away I got from that house, the better.

I hadn't known what to expect tonight when Lu had invited me to meet her family, but it hadn't been that.

I'd wanted her to be proud and excited to introduce me to her dad and stepfamily. That was why I'd given Jimmy my notice yesterday. It was time, and I was ready to move forward in my web design business, but I'd been stalling, using Huber as a backup.

But I didn't want Lu to have to introduce me tonight as her boyfriend, the ride-share driver. I knew how much she sought her father's approval. And when you didn't believe in yourself, other people wouldn't either. So I'd made the change.

Meeting my girlfriend's family for the first time was sure to be awkward as hell, but it was important to Lu. She wanted a perfect dynamic and better relationships with these people, so tonight had been important for me, too. I'd foolishly thought I could be a bridge, some new common ground to ease the tension Lu had lived with for so long.

But fuck. There was no coming back from this. Dated one daughter who was a certifiable monster. In love with the other, who was the best thing that ever happened to me. And I'd walked away from her because I'd been too mortified over my mistakes to let her help.

What a fucking mess.

I didn't know how far I made it before stopping at an intersection in a residential area and pulling out my phone. My breath came out in white puffs of frustration in the cold night air, and I was grateful that Lu hadn't come after me again. I couldn't think with her there. Couldn't put into perspective what a colossal fucking disaster I was when she was trying to make things right. I wouldn't be able to stand in her positive light right now, not when everything had gone to hell.

I was cold, and it was late, and my head pounded.

For the first time since coming to Cozy Creek, I called the rider request number for Huber. And ten minutes later, Jimmy pulled up in an old Chevy Impala looking like a knight in shining armor.

"Hop in, kid."

CHAPTER 16

Lu

I could hear Noah's boots scuffing along the pavement, but I kept my gaze firmly on my shoes.

"Stop pushing and pushing."

Tears welled in my eyes as he put more distance between us—as he hurried to get away from me and my fucked-up family.

"Forcing this isn't going to make it any better."

I blinked and my vision cleared until more moisture clambered to take its place.

Noah was right. I was guilty of pushing and pushing to get my way. I'd forced him into friendship by pretending my car was in the shop. He hadn't wanted anything to do with me when we first met. But I'd been selfish in wanting to get to know him. I thought I knew what was best for Noah, desperate to offer him friendship. I'd done whatever I could to paint Cozy Creek in the best light. I bent over backward to force my family into something I so desperately wanted. Even Cody thought I was incapable of giving up on Noah when he'd pushed me away after our first kiss. My friend had been right. I'd broken days later and texted Noah an opening that he hadn't taken. I was consistently strong-arming people into doing what I wanted. Never giving them room to breathe.

I was manipulative. No better than Ginny. And now we had the unbelievable connection of dating the same guy—hurting the same guy.

Noah was no longer visible on the roadside when I finally raised my head. He'd escaped and hadn't taken me with him. Even now, I itched to reach for my phone and call a ride for him. I didn't want him to be alone out in the cold. But I made myself resist. It wasn't my place. Noah was an adult and he had his phone with him. It wouldn't be right to assert myself once again just because I meant well.

I swiped the tears from my cheeks and turned back to the house. The driveway was empty. No one had even followed us out.

When I made it back into the warm kitchen, Ginny and Kimberly were in the middle of a conversation in the living room, and my dad was casually opening a bottle of wine. It was as if the scene from ten minutes ago never happened, like my boyfriend hadn't just abruptly walked out before meeting anyone.

"Everything okay, honey?"

I stared at my father. Hurt and disappointment swirled around me like bees buzzing. But through it all, anger rose to the surface. This family—and that was a loose approximation for it, really—might have cost me Noah. People who didn't really care about me, not in any meaningful way.

Sure, Noah was angry and overwhelmed right now. He'd pushed me away, but I understood why. He saw my well-intentioned manipulation for what it was. One more attempt to control and influence his life. And I didn't blame him for feeling blindsided by Ginny's presence here. He'd escaped like a cornered animal. I just wished he'd taken me with him.

"No, Dad. Everything isn't okay," I finally managed, voice thick and rough.

He set the bottle down with a click on the countertop.

I swallowed against the painful lump in my throat and admitted, "I can't keep doing this. Pretending that we're a happy blended family—trying to will it into existence so that I can maintain some sort of relationship with you." I looked at Kimberly. "Your wife tolerates me at best. She doesn't know anything about me and doesn't care to. She didn't even include me in your birthday dinner last month. I had to call the restaurant and add myself to the reservation."

My father frowned. "That can't be right, Lu."

Kimberly stayed quiet, and I nodded, knowing not to expect any more than that.

"Come on, Luanne. Grow up." Ginny's words drew my flat gaze. "You were practically an adult when your dad married my mom. No one expected us to be sisters or for my mother to have to raise you or something."

Naively, I'd thought my father and I were a package deal. Yet looking at Kimberly now, her brows lowered in confusion, I could see that she'd only ever married my father. She didn't plan on marrying me too.

I guess everyone thought I'd go off to college and move away, and then they could have their lives 2.0 free and clear. How unfortunate for all involved that I grieved my mother and tried to hold on to the meager offerings of a family I had left.

Kimberly might not be malicious in her intent, but I couldn't say the same for my stepsister.

"You're terrible," I told her calmly. "I'm tired of trying to force a family out of this shitty Cinderella re-telling. This isn't high school anymore, Ginny. Ironic that *you* are the one telling me to grow up. You still play the role of popular mean girl who needs to make me feel shitty about myself—my life and my job and even my name. I never once thought we could be sisters, but I tried for years to make us friends."

Before she could interrupt, I took a breath and said, "What you did to Noah was criminal. Cruel and vicious in a way I didn't think even *you* were capable of."

Kimberly shifted her attention to her daughter, and for the first time, suspicion entered her gaze. "What is she talking about, Ginny?"

Ginny shifted uncomfortably on her feet. But she could explain that herself. Or not. I didn't care. I was done with her. The way I should have been years ago.

There was nothing to save here. Noah had been right. I'd been the only one trying for a very long time, and it wasn't fair. Ginny wasn't even the sort of person I *wanted* in my life. If not for the connection between our parents, I would have hoped and prayed I never ran into her again after high school.

Kimberly . . . well, the jury was still out on her, but it wasn't looking good. Ginny was her daughter and her priority. She'd raised her, after all. If my stepmother wanted to make the effort to get to know me and really try to form some kind of relationship, I would be open to that. But I wasn't holding my breath. Not anymore.

However, if I could salvage one thing, it might be a future with my dad. A family didn't have to be the ideal I'd put on a pedestal. I didn't know why it had taken me so long to see that. Part of me felt like I was giving up—being a quitter. But what was the point in fighting for something when you were the only one willing to go into battle?

Finally, I turned to face my dad who, admittedly, appeared thunderstruck. "Dad, I would love to have a relationship with you someday," I said around the emotion clogging my throat, "but it's not going to be like this. Not anymore. I love you, and I want you to be happy. But this isn't healthy for me. If you want to know me, I'd like that. But you can't put down my job and my life, and you can't pretend that we're one big happy family."

"Lu," he called.

But I just shook my head. "My heart broke when Mom died,

and instead of helping me heal, you expected me to glue the pieces back together on my own. You made something new for yourself, and I get it. I really do. But there has never been a place for me here. It just took me a while to see it."

Reaching down, I grabbed my purse from where I'd dropped it. I took one more look around the room at the stunned faces staring back at me, and then I turned and left.

My instinct was to call Noah or just show up at his apartment.

But I didn't do that. I gave him the space he'd asked for. Part of loving someone was trusting them. And I did love Noah. I hoped I'd get the chance to tell him how much.

I wanted him to know that I didn't care who Ginny was to either of us. That he didn't need to feel shamed by our coincidental connection. But I imagined seeing her again and in such an unexpected way really messed with Noah's head.

So I would give him time to process.

Part of me thought I couldn't keep pushing with Noah. At some point, he'd have to make the choice for himself. And if he wasn't choosing me, I couldn't keep begging for scraps.

But I'd be here waiting when he was ready to talk.

Cody came over to keep me company on his night off. It was Monday, two days after the family dinner from hell. I had a text from my dad asking to talk when I was ready, but nothing from Noah so far.

"You want some of this Mongolian beef or no?" Cody held a white take-out carton in one hand and chopsticks clicked together in the other.

"Yes, please," I called and traded boxes with him, passing over the vegetable lo mein.

"I wish I was there," came a whiny voice from the laptop propped up on my toaster oven.

"We wish you were here too, Ems," I said.

"She means she wishes she was here to eat this food," Cody clarified.

Emma shrugged on screen, her blond topknot bobbing in agreement. "I haven't found a good place for Chinese takeout in Albuquerque."

Cody and I went back to piling rice and noodles and all manner of comfort food on our plates.

"That's what you get for moving away," Cody said without any sympathy whatsoever and then shoved half of an egg roll in his mouth.

Emma growled a little before turning her attention to me. "How're you doing, LuLu? Heard from Noah?"

I wiped a napkin across my mouth and ignored the spike of hurt that accompanied the subject change. "No, I haven't."

"That boy," Cody grumbled. "Looks like I'm going to have to trap you and Sad Boy Noah in a car again."

I shook my head. "You shouldn't have interfered and forced his hand in the first place. Noah asked for space, and I'm giving it to him. I'm not going to push him to do something he's not ready for. No more forcing things to get my way."

Glancing up from my plate, I saw Cody and Emma share a look, but I ignored them and went back to my pork fried rice.

"Lu, I know Noah said some hurtful things," Emma began.

"Some true things." I interrupted.

"But he was hurting and lashing out," she pointed out. "You don't manipulate people for your own pleasure."

"You're not a villain, LuLu," Cody tacked on.

"But he was right," I argued. "Look at how I wormed my way into his life. I got it into my head that he needed a friend, so I nominated myself for the position and made it happen. Lying about my car to accomplish my goal."

"You didn't lie exactly," Emma said gently.

"I was dishonest," I retorted. "And so wrapped up in what I thought was the right thing that I didn't even consider that Noah knew what was best for his own damn self."

"You really think hiding away and being Sad Boy elite until he could pick up and leave Cozy Creek was the best thing for him," Cody challenged.

I put my fork down with a clang. "That's not the point. I forced the issue and—"

"You didn't trick him into falling in love with you. He did that all on his own." Cody made an annoyed face. "Everything you did was to try to help him. That is the difference between good and bad here. Your intent. Look at what Ginny did. It was malicious and cruel. She intentionally set out to lure him in before she made her move. All you did was try to get him to go eat tacos with you."

"You're simplifying—"

"No. I'm not." Cody cut me off again, sharper this time. I could tell he was getting worked up. "People meet and fall in love in so many weird and wonderful ways. You and Noah just needed a chance. You never set out to hurt him, and your friendship grew all on its own after a while."

"No matter how it turned out, I'll always be sorry for how it started."

Cody abandoned his chopsticks and came over to me, his anger deflating at my watery tone. "I know what Noah said to you hurt. But, Lu, you don't strong-arm people or manipulate them to get your way. What you did with your family was try to get them to live up to your expectations. It was from a place of love. You gave them every opportunity, but they fell short. And now you're making your peace with it." My friend sighed. "And Noah. Think about how he must be feeling. It's awkward as hell to find out you dated your girlfriend's stepsister. He knows how badly you wanted a good relationship with Ginny—or at least something civil. Maybe he thinks he's driving a wedge between you two, and his presence will make your life with your dad and your stepfamily that much harder."

Oh. I hadn't considered that.

"He ran away because he was hurt," Emma said. "But maybe he's staying away because he doesn't want to hurt *you*."

I looked between my friends. "You think I should try to talk to him? But he told me to give him space."

"And you have," Cody agreed, rubbing a comforting hand up and down my arm. "But maybe you need to let him know that someone picked him for once. That he's not all alone in this town anymore and that you'd rather have his love than be constantly trying to earn it from your family."

I nodded.

"But, Lulu, you deserve someone who's going to pick you right back," Cody amended. "You're worth it."

"Thanks, Cody."

My friend was right. I could make the first move, but Noah had to want me and choose me himself. I couldn't make the same allowances all my life for people who made me work for their affection.

I thought about telling Noah what had happened after he'd left on Saturday with my family. I didn't know if he'd be proud or feel responsible. He might not want to hear from me at all.

But I could start small. Open the door a little so he could make his way through if he wanted to.

I picked up my phone off the countertop.

Cody nodded and Emma smiled.

And then hoped that I was doing the right thing for once.

CHAPTER 17

Noah

Lu: I just wanted you to know that I'm here for you, if you want to talk. Whenever you're ready. No pressure.

Me: Thanks. I just honestly have no idea what to say right now. When I figure it out, I'll let you know. Talk soon, Lumiere.

It had been two days since Lu texted, and I still didn't know what to say or how to make things right. I was still humiliated and dejected. But more than that, I felt like I was one more complication in Lu's life. Another roadblock on her path to having the family she wanted. Even if the sister she was hoping to form a bond with was a sociopath.

My feelings for Lu weren't really in question. I knew I loved her. What we had was special. She was beautiful and smart, and she had the biggest heart. There was no getting over her. She was my best friend.

Yet it was difficult to imagine a way forward. How did we manage a future together after what we'd discovered?

It was hard to envision holidays and get-togethers when you'd dated one hundred percent of the siblings present. Even if Lu could see past our unbelievable shared connection in the form of her stepsister, I doubted very much that her father could.

"Noah, you in or out?"

The deep voice of Cole Sutter dragged me up from the abyss of my current thoughts. It was Wednesday night poker at the firehouse. My third one. I probably still wouldn't be leaving with the shirt on my back especially seeing as how I was distracted by everything going on with Lu.

I cleared my throat and put my cards facedown. "I fold."

It was a small crowd. Only five of us played tonight in the second floor's common room amid bowls of snacks and sodas. The four other firefighters were on shift, and if a call came in, it would probably be doing me a favor to cut the night short. I didn't know why I'd agreed to come in the first place. I was in a shit mood.

But Cole and Pace were friends now, and I was getting to know the other guys as well. Staying home and wallowing on my night off hadn't held much appeal. Staring at my phone without knowing what to say wasn't getting me anywhere either.

They all shared a look as I settled back in my uncomfortable folding chair to watch the rest of the hand play out.

"You alright, man?" Jeff said from my right. He was a year younger than me and married to his high school sweetheart. They had a baby on the way.

I fought the urge to fidget. "Yeah, I'm good. Just not feeling particularly lucky tonight."

Three hands later, Cole threw a Sour Patch kid and hit me on the forehead. "What is going on with you? You're not even trying."

I stared at the horrible red candy on the tabletop and thought about Lu teaching me how to play. Lu teasing me. Lu propped up on the counter in her colorful kitchen.

Scrubbing a frustrated hand along my jaw, I admitted, "I don't know, man. I think the universe is out to get me."

Cole, Jeff, Pace, and Mason stared back at me expectantly. So I told them. I told them the whole shitty story. How I'd been dating someone online, lost my job, moved across the country only to discover I'd basically been catfished by a version of the girl I'd met on a dating app. When I got to the part about dinner at Lu's this weekend and the big reveal, they'd gasped like a bunch of middle schoolers.

"No way," Mason exhaled. His dark brows were high on his boyish face. This was his first year on the job, straight out of firefighter training, and something about having pity from the young rookie made me want to get out of here. But then he said, "Is Lu okay? Have you talked to her?" and I liked him that much more.

I shook my head. "Not really. She texted a couple of days ago to ask if I wanted to talk, and I told her I wasn't ready."

The deck and the game forgotten, Pace wondered, "Well, when do you think you'll be ready?"

"I don't know, man." Huffing a humorless laugh, I admitted, "It was pretty fucking embarrassing for one thing. Not to mention the reminder of how stupid I'd been to trust Virginia—Ginny—in the first place."

"You can't blame yourself for that, Noah." Cole's tone was serious. He abandoned the candy he'd been eating. "I went to high school with both of them. Ginny knew how to play people. Classic mean-girl, bullying bullshit. She manipulated teachers and parents, who all thought she walked on water. She was subtle in her malicious behavior. Even now, she's probably just bored with her life and using people like you to amuse herself. She was awful to Lu back then—starting rumors about her and filling her locker with tampons. Stupid shit like that. But Ginny was popular, and her stepdad was the principal. She was basically untouchable."

Knowing that she'd tormented Lu for over a decade was salt in the wound. Lu, the brightest light in any room, had obviously worked hard to forgive Ginny for her petty and spiteful behavior. She'd tried for years to forge some sort of familial relationship with her evil stepsister. My poor sweet Lu. She'd never deserved any of that.

Suddenly, I felt even worse because I had been taken in by such a terrible person. My insides twisted in the knowledge that I hadn't suspected a thing. Virginia had been a little self-involved and materialistic when we'd been together, but I hadn't seen what was right in front of me, and that stung.

"It doesn't make you stupid," Jeff added as if reading my mind. "It just means you have a shitty ex."

Pace regarded me with a mixture of pity and understanding. "Everybody has something in their past, Noah. You might think you know a woman, but they can still surprise you. And not always in a good way."

Mason cleared his throat and fidgeted with several of his poker chips. He took a deep breath and admitted, "My ex cheated on me for a long time, and I never knew it. Hell, we lived together, and I had no idea. I trusted her, and she had no problem lying to my face. Working long hours and girls' nights seemed like reasonable excuses, so I never questioned it."

"That's awful," I said quietly. "I'm sorry." I couldn't imagine living with someone—sharing your life like that—only to be betrayed.

Mason nodded. "It's okay. My future is out there somewhere. I'll find her."

"When did you live with someone, Mase? You're an infant. Was this high school?" Cole said, giving the younger man shit.

Mason held up his middle finger. "I'm twenty-two, old man. I've lived."

The others laughed and their lighthearted teasing even got a small smile out of me.

Cole jumped in with another example, "Madison is perfect"— we all groaned—"but a buddy of mine told me this story about a girl who set fire to her ex's motorcycle." All the first responders at the table shuddered.

I thought about what an ass I'd been to push Lu away on the side of the road, saying things that I knew would hurt her just so I could get her to back off. Maybe that arsonist had a good reason for what she'd done. I wouldn't blame Lu if she thought I deserved some payback. But instead, she was understanding and kind, and I hated myself a little more. I traced the outline of my phone in my pocket and thought about what to say to her—how to apologize for hurting her. She deserved so much better than me—better than her family and the hand she'd been dealt.

"Sorry," Jeff said around a mouthful of popcorn. "I have nothing to add. I found the love of my life in chemistry class my sophomore year. I'm a lucky bastard." He laughed and ducked as he got pelted by snacks from the others and my balled-up napkin.

Cole turned to me. "So what's the alternative? You going to break up with Lu over something that isn't even close to being her fault? You gonna leave town so you never have to risk running into Ginny Walker again?"

In the days since the dinner of doom, I hadn't let my brain land on any one solution. There wasn't a right answer that I could see through the fog of indecision. I didn't want to break up with Lu. I loved her and didn't want to give her up.

And Cole was right. Blaming her was a shitty thing to do. But causing more drama in her family felt selfish and wrong on every level. Not to mention, the thought of leaving Cozy Creek didn't sit right. There was nothing for me anywhere else, including my hometown. The truth was, this place was home now, and a big part of that was ... Lu.

"I don't know," I finally managed, feeling my frown deepen as my resolve waffled and my thoughts ping-ponged all over the place.

I finally had a life here in Colorado. I had another week and a half driving for Huber unless Jimmy hired my replacement sooner. My business was taking off. I had friends and felt settled despite my inauspicious beginnings in this tiny town.

And Lu was here.

"Don't let that psychopath run you off," Mason offered as he gathered the cards and started shuffling.

"And don't punish Lu for Ginny's mistakes," Pace added. "She doesn't deserve that."

Cole and Jeff nodded.

They were right. Lu didn't deserve my frustration or my shitty mood. She definitely didn't deserve me using her own fears against her. I never should have accused her of pushing me or forcing her hand. She'd only been trying to help, but I'd been too blinded by fear to allow it at the time.

The cards were dealt once more and I did my best to focus. I only lost *most* of the money I'd started the night with instead of all of it. But my mind was drifting down the path toward Lu and how I could fix things—how we could move forward after such a major surprise.

I still didn't know the right answer but I knew it wasn't something I could figure out without her.

CHAPTER 18

Lu

> Ride request for Luanne Billings. Please reply Y to confirm
> a pickup in 30 minutes.

I stared at Noah's text, as hope tried valiantly to take flight,
along with all the butterflies in my stomach.

Huber requests didn't typically work in reverse.

With a tentative finger, I replied with a capital Y and did my
best not to stare at the phone.

Noah's response was immediate: *Ride confirmed.*

It was midmorning, and I was supposed to be packing up orders to take by the post office later, but instead I was sneaking
peeks out my mini-blinds and wondering what was up. Was Noah
ready to talk?

When I caught a flash of blue turning into the Shady Peaks parking lot twenty-six minutes later, I put on my peacoat, slid into my ballet flats, and grabbed my purse off the couch before heading downstairs.

The Bronco was waiting by the curb.

"I'm here to pick up a Luanne Billings."

Noah wore a gray beanie and had the driver's side window rolled down. He was smiling at me. And maybe things were off between us right now, but seeing the warm expression on his face gave me hope for the first time since everything had gone so wrong at my dad's house, five days ago.

"That's me." My voice shook a little, but I managed a smile.

"Hop in, Bluey."

Another hopeful little token dropped in the bucket as I registered the nickname and teasing glint in Noah's eye. But I fought to lasso back my optimism before it got ahead of itself. He'd said he needed time, and I needed to moderate my expectations.

Gathering my things, I moved to the other side of the Bronco. I had a moment of hesitation on where to sit, but Noah leaned over and pushed opened the front door on the passenger side.

Climbing in, I couldn't help but stare. "What are you doing here?"

Noah made no move to drive away. We watched each other for a long moment, his hazel eyes drinking me in.

Carefully, Noah's hand slid into my hair. "I missed you so much. I'm sorry I needed some time to think. I'm sorry I pushed you away."

"It's okay," I said, moving to cup his hand with mine, holding it in place along my jaw. "I understand."

"I have a meeting we should get to. Then we can talk, yeah?"

I nodded numbly, wondering if he was breaking up with me. He wouldn't be looking at me like that if he was writing me off, right? Could he be planning on leaving Cozy Creek after all? A wave of uncertainty washed over me. And what meeting were we going to?

Noah's hand slid free from my tangle of hair, and he put the Bronco into drive.

It wasn't long before we were driving through a small residential neighborhood over on Firefly Lane. The houses were a little older; most were one-level ranch style with narrow yards and well-established trees. The house I'd grown up in with my mom was only a few streets over.

Noah stopped in front of a cute home with a large porch and a brick arch leading to the front door. The deep plum shutters looked freshly painted.

The *for sale* sign in the front yard drew my attention, and I stared at it for a moment before finally speaking. "I didn't know you were looking for a house."

"Will you come look at it with me?" Noah asked, voice careful and cautious, but there was a spark of something that sounded an awful lot like hope. "Then we'll talk."

The yard had a bright white picket fence around the perimeter, and we let ourselves in through the gate near the garage. We walked up the path to the front porch where a Black woman in her midforties waited in a killer pantsuit and wool coat. Her bright scarf lent a splash of color and set off her dark skin beautifully.

"Sorry we're late, Harriet," Noah apologized. "This is Lu Billings."

The woman smiled and slipped her cell phone into her coat pocket. "Hello, Lu. Nice to meet you." Her handshake was firm, and I was mildly off-balance to be strolling into this unknown situation.

But Noah gave me a warm smile and slid his fingers through mine.

When I glanced back to Harriet, she had the lockbox open and keys in hand. After ushering us inside, the woman who I now assumed was a real estate agent told us to have a look around the cozy three-bedroom and she'd be happy to answer any questions. "I'll be in the kitchen. I have a couple of phone calls to return."

Due to my confusion about what this all meant, I was grateful for the privacy and the permission to wander without a tour guide. The space was clean but empty.

Noah murmured quietly as we walked down the hallway, "It's been on the market for a little over four months. Harriet mentioned that the owners have already moved and were planning to lower the price on this place to avoid paying two mortgages."

I nodded though I didn't understand. My mind was racing. Was Noah staying? Did he want to live in this house?

The primary bedroom was decently sized, with large windows

facing the backyard and the mountains beyond. I had to admit that plenty of closet space and a newly remodeled bathroom were all nice touches. We wandered through to check out the two smaller bedrooms, and I couldn't hide my curiosity as I took everything in. Noah caught my questioning gaze and gave my hand a squeeze.

Eventually, we made our way to the kitchen. It was modest, but the appliances were all new, and I liked the open floor plan into the living room. But did it even matter if I liked this place? I wanted to drag Noah outside and make him explain what this all meant.

We reconvened with Harriet and Noah thanked her for her time, promising to be in touch soon. I stayed quiet as we headed back to the Bronco even though inside, my mind was going in a thousand directions, and only some of them good.

Noah started the car and turned the heat up, but we didn't go anywhere.

Eventually, he turned to look at me and I all but blurted, "What's going on, Noah?"

He reached for my hand again and laced his fingers through mine. "I wanted to have options when we finally spoke."

I frowned. "What options?"

"Someplace big enough for both of us. And maybe a dog. A decent yard to stretch out in. An office and storage space for DeLuLu Designs. Maybe a studio for you to work in too. I just wanted you to know that I was willing ... to make my life bigger, to include you. To stay. To build something together. That I'm *choosing* you. Choosing us."

I could feel my heartbeat in my chest, wild at what Noah was proposing. A life together. A future. Despite everything.

"You'd really stay in Cozy Creek? After what happened?" I ventured, almost too nervous to ask. It felt wrong to ask this of him, after everything.

He nodded.

"It's not too much? Too small?"

"For all my baggage, you mean?" Noah said simply, but his face was open—willing to have this conversation with me.

And for the first time all week, I could manage a deep breath.

"For all the reminders," I clarified. I'd made my home here because of my history and the memories of my mom, but I could understand choosing another home in spite of them too. Noah had the right to make that choice. And I would support him. I'd even go with him.

"I wouldn't ask you to leave," he replied. "You love it here, and your mom loved it here. Your . . . family is here. Your hometown means everything to you."

"Not everything," I admitted. "It doesn't mean more to me than you, Noah." A dozen emotions passed over his face, but I went on before he could say anything or object. "I can carry my memories of my mother with me anywhere. The place has never been the important part. And as far as my family, they had their chance. A lot of them, actually. It's time for me to do what's right for me."

Noah frowned in concern. "What do you mean?"

"After dinner the other night"—I cleared my throat, nervous to bring up what had happened before he did—"I went back in and let them know that I was done. I basically told Ginny to fuck off and that if Kimberly wanted to put in the effort to know me, then that was fine, but I wasn't killing myself for them anymore. You were right. I've been the only one trying, and it's not fair. I'm not doing it. I told my dad that if he wanted a relationship, it couldn't be on his terms any longer. Things would need to change. I left the ball in his court."

From the pained expression on Noah's face, he blamed himself. He confirmed it when he said, "Lu, I didn't mean to turn your family life into a *Jerry Springer* episode." His throat bobbed as he swallowed and looked away. "I moved here for your stepsister."

There it was. The knowledge that had blindsided him so ruthlessly and driven him away. The painful truth, the twisted turn of fate.

I reached for his hand, encouraging him to face me again. With my voice even and sure, I told him, "It was a coincidence, Noah."

He blew out a breath. "A fucking wild coincidence. A guy and two stepsisters."

"It's not your fault that our story started out like a porno."

Noah choked out a rough laugh, and I joined him. Sobering quickly, he begged, "How can you be so okay about this?"

"She got you here. She brought you to me." Emotion was creeping into my words and my tone, and I fought to keep tears out of my eyes. "And now that you're here, I don't ever want to lose you. You are my person, Noah. Ginny is . . . inconsequential.

She's not my friend, and she's not my family. I tried to make that happen for years. It's never going to. And it's not you driving a wedge between us. There was already too much history and hurt there. So stop blaming yourself."

I took a deep breath and squeezed the hand I still held—the hand I would hold for as long as he let me. "You gave me the strength to say what I've needed to say to my dad and his family for a long time. It was one thing to know that some nameless, faceless girl hurt you. But to know that it was *her* was the final nail in the coffin. I don't want anyone in my life who could ever be that cruel and conniving. I was already grasping at straws— for someone not worth my time or my energy. I could have probably forgiven the bullying and the terrible attitude. But knowing that she was the one who played games and lied to you . . . that is all I'll ever need to know about her. I can't forgive her for it. The truth is more important than the fictional future relationship I'd made up in my head anyhow. It doesn't hurt to lose that future because it was never real."

Noah's gaze dropped to my fingers intertwined with his. I could read the shame and self-loathing he wasn't able to hide, and I hated Ginny a little more as a result.

"But, Noah, it would kill me to lose you."

His head rose at my words, and I could see him struggling to accept the truth.

"We're real. This"—I lifted my hand and placed it over his heart—"you and me, we're real. You deserve to have someone pick you. I'd rather give you my love than people who don't deserve it. If you want it, that is."

Noah's hand came to rest over mine, the beat of his heart steady and sure beneath my palm. "I do. I do want it. You deserve to have someone pick you too, Lu. You're so good, deep down. You're my best friend, and I want to stay in Cozy Creek and be with you."

"I'm not going to give up on you." With a shaky smile, I admitted, "Maybe I do push—"

"No," Noah interrupted. "I'm sorry, Lu. So damn sorry. I never should have said that. I didn't mean it, and I have felt like utter shit since it left my mouth. I was punishing you for something that wasn't your fault, and I'll regret it forever."

"But you're not wrong." I smiled a little sadly. "I did push things with you. You didn't want to be my friend. I strong-armed you into hanging out with me. Using your job as a means to get closer and spend time together. Trying to make you want to stay in this town."

He was already shaking his head. "You didn't force me into anything. I wanted to know you. So badly. I just didn't trust myself. Every time your name popped up for a ride request, I could feel my stomach drop. I wanted to see you and spend time with you. I just wasn't brave enough to ask for it on my own. I'm glad you kept showing up. You haven't given up on me once. Even when I probably deserved it. I'm not ever going to be mad about you pretending your Jeep was in the shop. It's how I got to know you. It's how I fell in love with you."

I bit my lip as pressure built behind my eyes. The admission sent relief and joy coursing through my veins.

Noah sighed and smiled to himself, a little disbelieving. "Taking you on your first dates over and over again. Hoping and praying that each one would end in disaster so that I could be the one to take you home."

I grinned and leaned forward over the center console, desperate to hold him and touch him. His warm arms came around me, and I couldn't keep the words in any longer. "I love you, Noah."

His lips curved against the skin of my neck, and I felt the words take shape. "I love you, Luanne."

Smiling, I admitted, "I didn't hate it when you said it like that."

Noah's chest shook with quiet laughter before he let out a huge sigh. He must have felt the same mixture of relief and happiness that had settled into my bones.

Eventually, I pulled back from Noah's warm embrace, but he kept me close with a hand cupping my jaw.

"What do you think of the house?" His voice whispered and gaze went soft. "Could you see us here?"

I could. Even without knowing the context, I'd cataloged the things I'd loved on our walk-through. I'd seen the possibilities.

"I love it," I answered. "What do *you* think?"

"I think," Noah murmured, fingers combining gently through my hair, "that we're definitely going to need to paint those white walls. Give them some personality."

My smile stretched wide as I brought my lips to his, kissing for a future that was slowly coming into focus. I wanted this adventure with him—one which made my heart race and my breath catch.

Pulling back, I murmured against his lips, "I can't believe you did this. I can't believe you found a house and brought me to see it."

His nose nuzzled against mine sweetly, but his eyes remained closed. "I wanted you to know I was serious. That I meant it when I said I wanted to stay—that I wanted everything with you."

I nodded as emotion threatened once again, and I brought my mouth back to his.

As he deepened the kiss, my thoughts splintered into contentment and joy, a soul-deep rightness blanketing my heart.

Maybe I did hold on to things too tight—with both fists, kicking and screaming, and determined to keep them. But going forward, I would only be doing that with the things that mattered.

And Noah, he was worth fighting for. It turned out, I was too.

CHAPTER 19

Noah

I didn't mind Thanksgiving. It was actually my favorite holiday behind Halloween. Pie, deviled eggs, leftover turkey sandwiches. I was here for it.

But I could tell Lu was sensitive to the occasion with the changes happening in her life, namely the ultimatums she'd issued to her dad and stepfamily weeks ago.

We were attending the friends-and-family Thanksgiving luncheon at the Cozy Creek Lodge. The restaurant was closed until service this evening, but the owners let the restaurant staff invite relatives and close friends to celebrate the holiday in the fancy-schmancy dining room in the hotel, which was roped off from the public for the next few hours.

Lu and I thought it would be fun to attend as Cody's guests

and moral support. We briefly entertained the idea of spending Thanksgiving on our own, but part of me worried that Lu would feel her father's absence that much more if it was just the two of us.

Benjamin Billings had called Lu to invite her to Thanksgiving dinner at his house with Kimberly and Ginny—like nothing had changed. I wasn't sure if the man was in denial or nonconfrontational, but he hadn't made much effort to carve out a space for his daughter in his own life. Lu had politely declined, but I knew she was taking it hard.

So we were making the holiday a celebration and spending it with Cody and a whole dining room full of people—a lot of them were locals and residents, many of whom Lu was already well acquainted. I was determined to make sure she didn't miss out on anything. And I sincerely hoped her father got his shit together by Christmas.

Today, we planned to enjoy the luncheon and then hit the Cozy Creek Christmas Parade on Saturday. Megastar and Hollywood actor Grayson Ames was grand marshaling the event, and I figured I needed to see it to believe it. Plus, my buddies at the fire brigade were taking part, and Lu and I were nothing if not supportive.

"Does he always get so flustered when he talks to the head chef?" I whispered against the shell of Lu's ear.

"Oh yeah," she confirmed. "Cody has been crushing on him for years. It's the only time he lacks confidence. He becomes a totally different person."

I winced as Cody tripped over . . . air apparently, and then laughed awkwardly. "And clumsy, too. Yikes."

Cody turned, escape embarrassingly obvious on his features, and made his way toward us. Looking up, he saw us watching and made a face like he was in visible pain.

"It's okay. Don't freak out. Just come sit." Lu was already murmuring when Cody joined us at the table, his cheeks flushed pink. No, something brighter than pink. At this point, his skin would probably glow in the dark.

But instead of watching Cody struggle into his chair at our four-top table, my attention snagged on head chef, Gavin Wilson, who was staring after Cody with a wistful and resigned expression on his face that made me wonder if all of Cody's nervous energy and crush-worthy feelings were one-sided after all. Gavin visibly swallowed and turned to a young woman who'd arrived and put her arm through his.

"Is that his girlfriend?" I asked quietly.

Lu gave a discreet glance in their direction. Cody seemed unable to lift his mortified gaze from the tabletop as he gathered himself.

Finally, Lu replied, "No, that's his sister, Charlotte."

Lu rubbed soothing circles on Cody's upper back. "It'll be fine. You just need to figure out how to be yourself around him—your real self—and then he'll be helpless to resist."

"Yeah," I echoed. "You'll be shouting 'yes, chef' before you know it."

Lu glared incredulously at me, but Cody took a deep breath

and said, "Thanks, Noah."

I held up a hand for a high five, and he dutifully bro-slapped it despite a marked lack of enthusiasm.

Lu shook her head at us, but I smiled and kissed her cheek.

"Ew. None of that," Cody whined. "I cannot handle cutesy couple crap right now when I cannot even stand successfully in front of Gavin without making a fool of myself."

Standing, I said, "Come on, Cody. You'll feel better after you have some carbs."

Cody dragged himself to standing. "Thanks, Noah. You always know how to make me feel better."

Lu scowled, affronted. "Excuse me. You've known him all of—"

I shook my head and fought the urge to laugh as Lu looked on in annoyance. I put a reassuring arm around Cody's shoulders and guided him past her to the buffet.

I felt a sharp pinch on my backside and didn't even try to stop the grin that came over my face. If Lu was getting annoyed with me and focusing on Cody, then she wasn't thinking about her first holiday without her father. Maybe Thanksgiving lunch at the Cozy Creek Lodge would be a new tradition for us.

But hopefully next year, Cody wouldn't be such a sad sack about Gavin Wilson. Maybe by then, things would have turned themselves around. Only time would tell. Things were changing for Lu and me, too. You never knew what the future had in store. I hoped Cody's journey was one that brought him happiness though. The guy deserved it.

Lu and I had the house closing coming up soon. The owners had been eager for everything to go through, and the cozy three-bedroom ranch would be ours at the end of next week. We'd been spending our nights together anyway, but it would be nice to have one space that was ours instead of switching back and forth between our apartments. The house was the start of something new for both of us. I was ready, and I knew Lu was too.

"Noah!" Lu called, following the sound of the front door opening and closing. "Are you in here?"

I'd picked up the keys to the house this afternoon while she'd been at the first holiday market of the season selling her wares. I grinned as I thought about how she'd react if she heard me call them her wares again.

"In the living room," I finally answered, stepping out of the lime-green tent onto the hardwood floor.

The house was empty. The movers wouldn't be loading everything up until tomorrow, but we'd both been eager to visit the house on closing day.

Lu stopped short when she turned the corner into the living room and got a good look at the space. I'd picked up a two-person tent at the sporting goods store. It was set up with an air mattress and blankets inside. Bright flames crackled in the fireplace, and two camp chairs were arranged nearby, with a bag of Skytop Diner takeout sitting between them.

"Noah," she breathed, taking in the room.

"Welcome home, Lululemon."

Her gaze found mine, and she smiled. This bright, luminous thing that punched a hole in my chest and made me absurdly pleased to be the one who put it there. Her blond waves were trapped under a striped toboggan with a white puff ball on the top. Her tights were orange today and the friendship bracelets she wore for work peeked out from beneath the sleeve of her peacoat.

"I brought champagne. It's not cold, but I like this brand." She held up the bottle in her arms as proof. "Oh shoot. I forgot an opener."

I walked toward her and said, "Don't worry. I have a trick for that." Saw it on a Youtube video after some romance author couldn't get into her white wine.

She slipped her arms around me, cold from being outside. I thought I might like to be the one who warmed her up for the rest of our lives.

Chin tucked over my shoulder, Lu's voice emerged unsteady. "I can't believe you did all this."

My arms squeezed a little tighter. "I thought it would be fun."

And it would be, with Lu. She was my best friend and made any situation better just by being there. We had fun together. Happiness wasn't some elusive thing I was chasing anymore nor was it a looming threat I expected to abandon me at any moment. My life with Lu was joy, plain and simple.

I wasn't naive enough to think there wouldn't be hard times or disagreements or miscommunication. We were people, not robots. We weren't immune to bad moods and necessary compromise. Relationships would never be totally perfect—that was unrealistic. But she and I were in this, committed to loving each other and listening to each other every day.

I was done questioning my better judgment or the luck that had fallen into my lap. I was going to hold on to Lu just as hard as she was holding on to me.

"This is our house," she sort of squeaked against my neck.

I grinned into her riot of hair, tugging off the toboggan in the process. "This is our house," I confirmed. "We can leave the Christmas lights up till January."

She giggled and leaned back to look at me. "Okay, show me this tent. Survival skills are important, and I need to make sure you're a proficient partner."

"Well, it's a little late for that. You're stuck with me. But please direct your attention to the fire I made."

Lu peered around me. "Those are gas logs."

"Yes, but I had to light the pilot, and it made that scary whoosh sound when I turned on the gas."

She shook her head but I could tell she was trying not to laugh.

Leaning down in front of the tent, I unzipped the flap and the netted layer and tied them back so she could climb in.

Lu set down the sparkling wine and her body bag purse, shucked her peacoat and her boots, and climbed inside. "Ohhhh," she said, voice echoing and impressed from inside the tent. "This is cozy."

"Champion hunter-gatherer right here."

"Come on over. Let's make sure we both fit."

She didn't need to tell me twice. I found her lying on her back, arms behind her head as I ducked in and climbed up the inflatable mattress. I hovered over her, arms and legs straddling the line of her petite body.

Lu grinned wickedly and wrapped herself around me, drawing me in for a kiss. "It's awesome. I love it. Thank you."

"Good," I murmured, placing an open-mouthed kiss along her jaw. "I want to make you happy."

Cupping my cheeks, she brought my attention back to her face. Her smile had softened, and she gazed at me with sincerity shining in her beautiful gray eyes. "You're doing pretty good so far."

She brought her lips to mine as her quiet, earnest affection seeped into my bones.

Slowly and carefully, I lowered my body to hers. Lu spread her thighs wide as I settled my hips between them. The air mattress shifted as I pressed myself fully against her.

My fingers drifted into her hair as they often did, seeking that wildness that I loved so much. Lu's hands worked their way beneath my hoodie, leaving gooseflesh in their wake as her nails scraped up and down my torso. With some careful maneuvering and shaking nylon, she managed to get my shirt over my head and my jeans unbuttoned.

"Shit," I hissed when Lu's clever fingers wrapped around my length, hard as fucking stone inside my boxer briefs. Before I could even blink, she'd produced a condom from somewhere and was sliding it on. We worked together to get her orange tights and underwear off without throwing one of us off the unstable mattress.

Somehow, Lu ended up shirtless on top of me, her corduroy skirt still on and bunched up around her waist. Her bra was another sheer number that made her nipples look pink and lickable. She rocked over me, hot and wet and entirely mine. The sensation of her sinking deep onto my cock had my eyes rolling back as I thought *more* and *God* and *fuck, yes.*

With a hand on her back, I urged her to lean forward so I could suck on her tits through the delicate fabric of her bra.

I was never going to get enough of this girl. She would be the center of my universe until the day I died. Whatever path—whatever journey—we were on, we'd take it together.

Visions of the future danced behind my eyelids amid sparkling lights as we moved together. Birthdays and holidays. Watching Lu from across whatever room we were in. Celebrations with friends. Movie nights on a blue velvet sofa. Working side by side in our home, me on a laptop and Lu at an easel. The Cozy Creek Fall Festival every year. Us in the fenced-in yard with a dog. Painting every room in this house to make it our own. Turning that third bedroom into a nursery when the time was right. Thinking up a new nickname every single day for the rest of our lives.

Blond hair fell all around us as Lu brought her lips back to mine, urgent and broken as her breathing spiraled. She was getting close, and I was hanging on by a thread.

We were tucked away in our own little world. The only thing I could see was her. Her on the sidewalk, waiting for the Bronco and jolting me back to life. Lu in my back seat, red lips laughing and hair blowing in the wind. The absolute comfort of her beside me, in the dark, in the light, consuming my thoughts and burrowing so deep inside my heart, she'd never get out.

"Noah, look at me," Lu breathed, voice rasping softly against my kiss-swollen lips.

I emerged from a dream where the future and past swirled and collided. We locked eyes as the world broke apart around us—shimmering bright and bold in the present tense, this woman I loved held tight in my arms.

Lu settled on her side next to me as we both worked to catch our breath. I needed to get up and take care of the condom, but I also needed a minute to get my bearings. Lu's fingernails stroked gently over my chest. I pressed a kissed to her damp forehead.

She hummed sweetly against me, content, before saying, "I'm glad you thought of the tent."

My eyes were drifting closed against my will. "Why is that?"

"Because we don't have curtains yet, and *that* was not how I envisioned meeting our new neighbors."

My laughter was a warm weight inside me. Or maybe it was Lu and that sunlamp glow she always made me feel. "And by *that* you mean . . . "

She shifted, and the air mattress dipped again. "You know, topless and riding you in the living room."

I cracked an eyelid. She was propped on an elbow, grinning

down at me.

"Ah, yes. *That*," I murmured, turning and burying my face in her neck.

Lu squealed and laughed as I tickled her, the mattress shaking and jolting us together. She couldn't get away.

After a moment, she braced her arms against mine and wheezed out, "Wait." I paused as she arched to get a better look outside the tent flap. "Do I smell burgers and tots from Skytop?"

Rolling flat on my back, I closed my eyes and groaned. Now I'd lost her. "Maybe."

She peppered kisses all over my face. It was her turn to tickle me with blond waves cascading everywhere. "Thank you, Noah. You're so good to me."

I wanted to argue and say it was *her* that was good to me. Far better than I ever deserved. It had been Lu who'd been patient. Lu who'd brought me back to life. Lu who'd put her faith in me. Lu who'd forgiven me.

But I knew she wouldn't tolerate any one-sided claims, so I spoke the bigger truth. "We're good to each other."

She grinned. "Yeah, we are, beekeeper." She delivered one last lingering kiss before she said, "Now, let's go eat some burgers."

And so, we did.

It seemed to be a fitting first meal for our life together in our new home. It had been the thing that started it all. I would always be grateful for that blind date who'd stood Lu up all those months ago. And for every douchebag who'd missed out on the best person they never got a chance to know. Because she was mine and I was hers.

It started with a phone call and a ride request. A twist of fate in an unexpected place.

I was just glad she was driving off into the sunset with me.

EPILOGUE

The New Year's Eve celebration in downtown Cozy Creek was in full swing when Noah and I arrived.

Despite the cold and the snow on the ground, children were bundled up and dashing around with sparklers. Main Street was all lit up and festive with its black and silver decorations. I was wearing some highly impractical sequin-studded shoes for the occasion. But sometimes you just had to wear the shoes.

In a lot of ways, the upcoming new year felt like a new beginning. One I was ready to welcome with open arms.

Noah's fingers laced through mine, and I shot him a bright smile. The one I got in return made my stomach flip.

We'd been living together for almost a month now, and things were going great. True to his word, we'd painted every room in the new house to make it a bright and cheerful home that I loved. His one demand was hanging his *Live Laugh Love* painting above his desk in our shared office. We'd gotten used to being in each other's space, and I had to admit, Noah was a good roommate. We were even talking about adopting a dog in the spring.

The upcoming year had me feeling hopeful. Change was a necessary part of life, and sometimes those changes took your breath away.

Tonight's festivities included the grand opening of the Lily Carmichael Memorial Gallery. I was happy to support Lily's son, Levi, who'd chosen to honor his late mother with a fitting memorial as well as display her amazing photographs for all to see and experience. Lily had been a loving staple in Cozy Creek and a gifted photographer. And she'd been taken far too soon and was greatly missed by the community.

When I'd contacted Levi and expressed interest in occupying a tiny corner of his gallery with my artwork, he'd been all for it. And tonight—for the first time in a very long time—I'd get to see my original paintings displayed at an art venue.

I was slowly dipping my toes back into creating. For so long, I'd pushed that part of myself to the wayside in favor of the business side of things—the lucrative and efficient side of things. But despite what my dad always presumed, I *did* have enough room for that side of myself. The parts that enjoyed painting and our beautiful surroundings, the mountains, and the places my mom had loved. It was another way I could keep her in my heart, and I liked to think that she would support me in painting again.

I still had DeLuLu Designs. That was my business and my baby. It wasn't going anywhere. Now, I simply made time for myself to create and to have fun with it.

The paintings displayed this evening would be available for purchase, and Levi seemed to think the tourist population would be excited for the opportunity to take a piece of Cozy Creek home with them. I was trying to feel brave about putting myself out there, but nerves were creeping around the corner.

"Whoa," I breathed, catching sight of the crowd in front of the gallery.

I slowed as we approached, and Noah glanced back. "Everything okay?"

Clearing my throat, I managed, "Yeah, just surprised at the turnout."

"I'm not. Want me to announce that my girlfriend is a featured artist and to get out of the way?"

"God, no," I said, tugging his arm. But then I looked at the grin on his handsome face and realized he was joking.

After a moment, we waded into the crowd, and Noah leaned down. With his lips by my ear, he whispered, "It's going to be great. I just know it, Lu-onardo Da Vinci."

Something tight in my chest loosened a bit as amusement wormed its way in. I pulled back to eye him. "That was ... "

"Kind of a stretch." Noah grinned. "I know. I'm workshopping others. How about Pablu Picasso?"

I laughed, another band of unease snapping in the face of Noah's playful distraction.

"Frida Kahlu?"

"Oh my gosh," I exclaimed, but I was still laughing.

And then we were inside the open gallery doors and I loved Noah for a million different reasons—another one joining the list as he worked to put me at ease, making me feel supported and cared for and so damn grateful. I felt unbearably lucky to have him here tonight.

My phone buzzed rapid-fire inside the pocket of my skirt. I pulled it out to find a string of texts from Cody.

Cody: Just got off work.

Cody: I'll be down the mountain in twenty.

Cody: I have my name tag ready to go: Best Friend to the Artist

I rolled my eyes but couldn't help but grin.

Another buzz.

Cody: Save me a glass of champagne.

I was much more relaxed as we eventually made our way fully into the gallery. Levi had done a great job rehabbing the downtown storefront in the last few weeks. It was all elegant lines and a bright, welcoming space—exactly what Lily Carmichael would have wanted.

We spied the new business owner and his girlfriend, Claire, who I'd heard all about on the Cozy Creek grapevine. I was eager to introduce myself, but I wasn't about to elbow my way over there and interrupt the way those two were looking at each other.

Noah got some back slaps and *hey, mans* from several fire brigade members, including Pace Leigh. Cole Sutter was also in attendance, with a stylish Madi Winslow on his arm. Cole's two adorable children looked excited to be up past their bedtime. I grinned at what a gorgeous family they made.

Noah snagged two champagne flutes as we worked through the crowd. We checked out Lily's permanent collection of photographs as well as other local artists who'd chosen to display their work on the gallery walls. All types of media were represented, including some of Levi's amazing woodworking sculptures on pillars.

Eventually, we turned the corner to the area I knew housed my collection of landscapes, but I nearly stumbled at the picture waiting for me.

My dad was standing in front of my pieces. His thinning brown hair and wool dress coat were so familiar yet so distant that I felt myself rooted in place, emotions going haywire.

Since I'd given my dad and stepfamily my ultimatum back in November, my dad kept acting like nothing had changed. He'd invited me to spend the holidays—Thanksgiving and Christmas—with him and Kimberly and Ginny like my angry breakdown in his kitchen had never happened. And I'd responded to each text politely and declined each time. He'd made no effort to meet me on neutral ground. So I'd assumed he'd made his decision, choosing to fully embrace his new family in favor of all that was left of his old one.

Seeing him in the gallery, in front of my paintings, was off-putting and confusing.

And I definitely hadn't expected him to show up here tonight with no clear invitation from me—to support something that he'd done his best to minimize and talk me out of my whole life. He'd always insisted I use my art and design degree to teach. I understood a father wanting security and success for his daughter, but my love for art—for the sake of art—had never been something he could wrap his head around.

"Dad?"

He spun at my question. With a finger extended, he pointed at the painting on the left. It was a night landscape, all dreamy midnight blues with inky shadows for mountains, the snow on the peaks gleaming in the ethereal moonlight, and the bright stars sparkling in the sky amid shades of violet. "That's Coleman Overlook."

I nodded, feeling the confused frown overtake my features.

"Your mom loved it there."

"I know," I replied quietly. "I still visit."

"You do?" His expression spoke of surprise and sadness. My father had wanted to separate his life cleanly, a hot knife dividing his time with my mother to before and after her death. Maybe it was hard to imagine he'd raised a daughter who willingly and deliberately held on to the things he'd been desperate to let go of in his grief.

"I do," I confirmed, voice close to breaking. "I even took Noah there."

"Noah," he repeated as if just now noticing the silent, watchful man at my side. With surprising speed and recovery, the finger he held aloft toward the painting transitioned to an outstretched hand. "It's, um, nice to meet you, son. I apologize for the way—"

"It's okay," Noah said quickly, cutting him off. He returned my father's gesture before bending close to me. "I'll give you a minute to talk."

"No, stay," my dad interjected. "I wanted to talk to you both. To tell you I was sorry, and that I'd like very much to be in your lives. To make the effort." He turned watery eyes on me. "To get to know you both better."

Noah always claimed I had a forgiving heart. And maybe my dad wasn't perfect, but he was here, and he was trying. I had to hope he'd stand behind his claims. It wasn't so much forgiveness as wanting my dad back. But I was done settling for the bare minimum. So I didn't rush to reassure him, and I didn't throw my arms around him.

With careful deliberateness, I said evenly, "I'd like that, Dad."

I could have asked about Kimberly, but her absence was indication enough. And I didn't want to start something that would take away from this night—one I was proud to be a part of and celebrate accordingly.

My father ushered me forward, heedless of the people crowding around for a better look. He asked me about the other landscapes on display and wanted to know about the areas I'd painted. I discussed my process—the sketches I made from life and the color studies I did in person. Others in the crowd realized I was the artist at some point and joined in with their praise and

questions. I was so deep in answering thoughtful, curious inqui-
ries from both strangers and my father alike that I didn't notice
the sold stickers beside each title plaque until Noah tilted his
head in the direction of one.

Pride and joy swelled somewhere deep inside. I hadn't set out
to make money or a name for myself, and I likely never would.
I'd simply been eager to acknowledge the part of my heart I'd
ignored for many years. Validation wasn't necessary but it did
ignite a tiny spark that had me staring in wonder at those little
stickers.

When I'd gone quiet, and my father had gone back to staring
at the Coleman Overlook painting, Noah dipped his head and
pressed a kiss to my temple. "I'm so proud of you."

I turned and caught his surprised lips unaware. "I love you,
Noah," I said softly after pulling away. "Happy New Year." I was
so grateful for his unexpected arrival in my very ordinary life all
those months ago.

His hazel eyes were warm swirls of brown and green that never failed to draw me in. "I love you back. So much. I can't wait to
spend every new year with you."

And what a future it was shaping up to be.

Want more Noah and Lu? Check out a bonus scene for Fall Me Maybe *when you sign up for Laney's newsletter!*

Scan the QR code to get your bonus scene:

THE COZY CREEK COLLECTION

Fall I Want by Lyra Parish
Fall at Once by Nora Everly
Falling Slowly by Enni Amanda
Fall Too Well by Erin Branscom
Fall Shook Up by Piper Sheldon
Fall Me Maybe by Laney Hatcher

www.cozycreekbooks.com

ABOUT THE AUTHOR

Laney Hatcher is a firm believer that there is a spreadsheet for every occasion and pie is always the answer. She is an author of stories both old and new where the HEAs are always guaranteed. Often too practical for her own good, Laney enjoys her life in the southern United States with her husband, children, and incredibly entitled cat.

Find Laney Hatcher online:
Facebook: https://bit.ly/3s6KnuY
Newsletter: https://bit.ly/3SbXg2v
Amazon: https://amzn.to/3IaOwU7
Instagram: https://bit.ly/3s4IRcS
Website: https://laneyhatcher.com/
Goodreads: https://bit.ly/3BD0Gme
TikTok: https://www.tiktok.com/@laneyhatcherauthor
Threads: https://www.threads.net/@laney.hatcher

Newsletter Sign-up

ALSO BY LANEY HATCHER

BARTHOLOMEW SERIES

First to Fall: A Friends to Lovers Historical Romance

Second Chance Dance: An Enemies to Lovers Historical Romance

Third Degree Yearn: A Second Chance Historical Romance

Last on the List: A Surprise Pregnancy Historical Romance

KIRBY FALLS SERIES

Take It or Leaf It: A Grumpy Sunshine Small-Town Romance

SMARTYPANTS ROMANCE

LONDON LADIES EMBROIDERY SERIES

Neanderthal Seeks Duchess: A Smartypants Romance Out of this World Title

Well Acquainted: A Smartypants Romance Out of this World Title

Love Matched: A Smartypants Romance Out of this World Title

Find bonus content, reading order, and other news at my website:
https://laneyhatcher.com

Milton Keynes UK
Ingram Content Group UK Ltd.
UKHW041315290824
1429UKWH00076B/1939